Nelson had been acting strangely ever since his near-death experience, and Hurley, too. The two of them were covering something up, something that Rachel Mannus would encounter tonight, unless Labraccio got there in time.

If only Rachel hadn't been so stubborn! He had to stop her before she went under. He had to bring her back before she, too, became the target for whatever it was that was waiting out there for them.

David ran swiftly across the marble floor of the rotunda, not caring whether anybody heard his footsteps, down the corridor, and into the Dog Lab.

Rachel was lying still and deathly pale on the gurney, and the monitors showed only flatlines.

COLUMBIA PICTURES Presents A STONEBRIDGE ENTERTAINMENT Production

A JOEL SCHUMACHER Film "FLATLINERS"

KIEFER SUTHERLAND JULIA ROBERTS KEVIN BACON

WILLIAM BALDWIN OLIVER PLATT Music by JAMES NEWTON HOWARD

Editor ROBERT BROWN Production Designer EUGENIO ZANETTI Director of Photography JAN DE BONT

Executive Producers SCOTT RUDIN MICHAEL RACHMIL PETER FILARDI

Written by PETER FILARDI Produced by MICHAEL DOUGLAS RICK BIEBER

Directed by JOEL SCHUMACHER

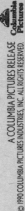

Columbia
Pictures

DOLBY STEREO
IN SELECTED THEATRES

FLATLINERS

a novel by
LEONORE FLEISCHER

based on the motion picture written by
PETER FILARDI

TOR®

A TOM DOHERTY ASSOCIATES BOOK
NEW YORK

This is a work of fiction. All the characters and events portrayed in this book are fictitious, and any resemblance to real people or events is purely coincidental.

FLATLINERS

Copyright © 1990 by Columbia Pictures Industries, Inc.

A Tor Book
Published by Tom Doherty Associates, Inc.
49 West 24th Street
New York, N.Y. 10010

Cover art © 1990 by Columbia Pictures Industries, Inc.

ISBN: 0-812-51188-3

First edition: July 1990

Printed in the United States of America

0 9 8 7 6 5 4 3 2 1

FLATLINERS

PROLOGUE

The idea had first burrowed its way into his head years ago. He was twelve years old then, a strange, troubled, precocious child with an overactive imagination and no friends. Spending many hours alone in the institution library, never reading, never playing or listening to music, he would sit at the keyboard of the one PC they had for three hundred youngsters, and ask it unanswerable questions, punching the keys furiously and scowling at the screen.

"What is the nature of life?" he'd demand of the computer, but the machine stayed silent. "Will evil win out over good?" "Is there a God?" "Do other planets have intelligent life?" And the most anguished questions of all, "What happens after you die?" and "Why can't I live forever?"

If the computer did know the answers, it wasn't telling him. There was no software program in any of the thick catalogs that could make it tell, no key code that he could find to penetrate the PC's secrets. Staring at the screen until he was almost blind, his strange pale-green eyes would be luminous with desperation, his yellow hair rumpled and dark with sweat, anger contorting his soft boyish features.

Until, exhausted at last, feverish and frustrated, he would capitulate to the computer's mocking silence, and turn away to yet another elaborate game of *Dungeons and Dragons*, in which he played all the roles and held all the weapons and the powers and the mystery.

But at night, alone in a crowded dormitory room in his terrifying childhood bed, an ustable island in a volcanic sea of monsters, his thoughts would center reluctantly on death—hating it, fearing it, bitterly resentful of its inevitability. Someday even he would be forced to lie alone and abandoned in the damp earth, his flesh mouldering off his bones, his hair and toenails continuing to grow as the precious reality that had once been himself was transformed into an unseeing, unfeeling, unknowing skeleton. It was a thought that the boy couldn't avoid thinking, even though it literally nauseated him.

He pictured life as an endless conveyor belt, with everybody in the world standing on it in a single line, in the order in which they were to die. Little children and old people, strong young men and women, all mixed in together, linked only by the hour of their death. And the conveyor belt kept carrying them along, inexorably, never stopping, never even slowing down. When the conveyor belt of life reached Grand Death Station, it dumped its passengers off. Without ceremony, without reprieve, without a return ticket. And that was all she wrote.

But what if death was not the last waltz after all? What if there was something out there, something more? What if someday he himself would be the first to go and have a look-see; to come back with the answer the world had been searching for since earliest man? Death couldn't be final. There was something else waiting out there. There had to be. The entity that was him couldn't simply come to an end, just like that, snuff. It didn't make sense. It was too much of a waste.

Someday he'd go and have a look-see. . . .

—— CHAPTER 1 ——

Last night the emergency room had been even more chaotic than usual, as blackly terrifying as the third circle of Dante's Hell. Maybe it was because the moon was full, a huge burnished dark-orange circle hanging low in the sky, the harvest moon of late October, which calls up Hallowe'en lunacy. Maybe it was the moon, or maybe it was only a sudden increase in the volume or toxicity of street drugs, but last night the ER had been packed solid with incoming assault victims, everything from a fractured tibia to a slashed jugular.

Even today, with the night shift dragging to an exhausted close and the first pale sun-streaks coming in through the barred windows, there was no letup in the emergency caseload. Too many patients, not enough time, not enough nurses, not enough doctors. There wasn't even the leisure to practice triage today; patients in pain had to be left alone to plead for help on gurneys in the corridor outside the ER, then grabbed up as soon as possible and rushed screaming into cubicles. Sometimes their lives were saved. Sometimes not. After a while, the interns said, you get used to the screaming and the pleading, and even to the blood. There was always blood in the ER, blood gushing violently from gunshot wounds, pouring out of stab wounds, dribbling from self-inflicted cuts and slashes.

David Labraccio knew he'd never get used to the blood. Not that he was squeamish—no third-year medical student could afford to be—but he was always too aware of how precious the red liquid was to life, and to see it draining away like dirty wastewater always cut him to the heart.

This Hispanic woman's blood was draining fast. Her abdomen, legs and thighs were covered thickly in it; blood had seeped through her clothing and soaked through to the gurney on which she lay writhing and moaning in the corridor, waiting for one of the curtained-off cubicles. In contrast to the vivid red of her vital fluid, her face was a chalky white. Labraccio looked around in desperation. The ER was overcrowded, but not a doctor was in sight. Only a harried nurse, an orderly and himself, a third-year medical student, and all that blood.

"Blood pressure sixty plus and dropping," muttered the orderly, as David seized the gurney and began rolling it into the ER. "My God, she's going!"

"Vaginal bleeding?" Labraccio asked, and the nurse nodded.

The woman's common-law husband was in hysterics, sobbing in Spanish, wild words pouring out of him as he watched his wife dying in front of his eyes.

"What's he saying?" Labraccio demanded of the Venezuelan orderly.

"No money . . ." the orderly replied. "Jesus, probably a street abortion."

Unless something radical was done immediately, the woman was going to bleed to death. David Labraccio made a quick decision. "Probably severed the femoral artery. We have to open her up. Do a midline."

The nurse shook her head grimly, her brow furrowed. "The surgeon won't be out of OR for another ten minutes," she pointed out.

Impatiently, David shook his head, and his thick dark hair flopped over his eyes. He wasn't about to just stand there and let this woman die.

"Too late," he barked. "Get her under."

"Who's gonna do the surgery?" demanded the nurse.

But Labraccio was already pulling on a pair of surgical gloves and picking a scalpel up from the tray of instruments. "I am."

The nurse let out a little gasp of horror. A

medical student, not even a graduate doctor! No way! It was totally out of the question! "You can't . . ." she began to protest, but Labraccio cut her off curtly.

"Do it!" he barked, and his youthful face held such authority that the nurse gave up protesting, and placed an anesthesia mask over the shrieking woman's face.

David pulled up the woman's bloody clothing, baring her belly. At the sight of her naked skin and the scalpel in the young man's hands, her husband's yelling began to escalate.

"Get him out of here, now!"

Without hesitation, the orderly obeyed, ushering the frantic man out of the cubicle at the exact moment that David Labraccio sliced firmly into the woman's abdomen, plunged his right hand into the gaping incision, and groped among her intestines.

"Where is it? Where is it?" he muttered to himself as he searched for the source of all that bleeding. Finding the severed artery, he grabbed it tightly, cutting off the gushing flow of blood.

"Clamp!" he yelled, and the nurse slapped one into his left hand. Bending over the unconscious woman, David clamped the artery shut. The bleeding stopped, except for the seeping around the incision itself.

"What the hell is going on here?"

Two doctors came running down the corridor, tipped off by one of the ER nurses. One of them angrily elbowed Labraccio aside. "Dave, get outta here! Now!"

Reluctantly, David Labraccio backed into the corridor, his eyes still fixed on the patient.

"All right, I got it. Let's get her into OR," the surgeon instructed the nurse, and the two of them rushed the gurney out of the cubicle, the nurse still attaching the intravenous tube as they ran.

The other surgeon, Dr. Miriam Bernbohm, turned angrily to David Labraccio. "What the hell do you think you're doing?" Her voice was pitched low, but the anger in it was almost palpable.

"Saving her life," retorted David defiantly, his lips taut, but his hands trembling a little.

"You're a student, not a doctor!" Bernbohm reminded the boy harshly.

Labraccio's eyes blazed with indignation. The words came tumbling out of his mouth before he had a chance to think. "It was an emergency. None of you were available. If I hadn't done a midline, she would have died in another twenty seconds!"

"You're not licensed to do any surgical procedure," snapped the surgeon coldly. "She could have died and the insurance companies would have dangled this hospital and this university by a thin thread. That's why we keep students away from sharp objects!"

Taking a deep breath, Dr. Bernbohm willed herself into calmness, studying the serious face of the defiant young man who stood in front of her in a set of blood-soaked greens. She knew little about this year's crop of medical students, but she knew that David Labraccio was a standout among them, an excellent technician whose grades showed real promise and whose hands were the hands of a surgeon. Bernbohm could see and—even if the boy didn't believe it— actually appreciate the commitment and pure passion for healing behind Labraccio's impulsive act. The young man's instincts were those of a doctor—human life was precious to him.

Nevertheless, David Labraccio had to be made an example; an incident like this could not go unpunished, or discipline in the med school would begin to disintegrate. It was time that David Labraccio began to learn some of the grown-up logistical complexities of life-saving.

"I'm afraid I have no choice but to recommend your suspension," she said slowly. "You can reapply next summer for the fall term, but I can't guarantee that your scholarship will be renewed." Turning abruptly, the surgeon walked away.

David glared after Dr. Bernbohm's retreating back; his breathing was hard and his hands, still in their bloody surgical gloves, were clenched into fists.

"Don't worry about it!" he yelled angrily. "There's no sense in my reapplying. If the situation ever arose again, I'd do the same thing!"

But underlying the boy's righteous anger was a gut-wrenching uneasiness. He was scared, scared good. Suspended, Jesus! What could he tell his parents? What would become of his medical career? What the hell was he going to do now?

The late October winds off Lake Michigan held the icy promise of an early winter, but in the thin patches of pale sunlight between the buildings the air was crisp and golden. Autumn melancholy sent dry leaves of yellow, red and brown skittering across the campus quad to gather in rustling banks against the dark brick walls of the university.

Nelson Wright put his hand up to his face and adjusted his Vuarnet shades. Even the faintest sunlight was hard on his pale eyes, often sending shock waves of pain stabbing through his forehead. He shivered a little in the icy dawn, and pulled his long green woolen coat around his thin frame, drawing the belt tighter.

The lake was choppy this morning, thanks to the wind. It lapped against the shoreline as though it was taking little wet nibbles out of the land. The rising sun sent its feeble rays slanting westward over the gray water. The sky was very blue; the air cold but very fresh.

Nelson smiled. He loved this time of day, the hour of solitude, before the campus was swarming with pushing, yelling, socializing young people on their way to class. He liked the feeling of being the sole lord and owner of his surroundings. The cold morning, the empty quad, the sleeping buildings—all these belonged to Nelson Wright. Especially today.

Rocking back on his heels with his hands deep in his overcoat pockets, Nelson took a deep breath, smelling the lake, the dusty leaves under his feet, the winy air, and anything else that was out there waiting just for him.

"Today is a good day to die." He grinned.

Making his way briskly across the quad, Nelson kept his head down until he was very close to the Taft building. This classical structure, with its famous sculptural program and glassed-in rotunda roof, was a laboratory building attached to the med school. Over eighty years old, Taft was finally undergoing renovations and was therefore temporarily closed to the students and the public. Warning signs had been posted all along the building's walls:

CLOSED FOR REMODELING
NO ADMITTANCE

Behind its Grecian columns and under its Roman pediment, Taft's large bronze front doors were chained shut and the windows were boarded up. Only a small side door, through which the construction crews came and went, had been left unchained; but the door was always kept locked and only the foreman of the renovation workers had the key.

Nelson Wright raised his head and looked around carefully. Nobody in sight. Good. Moving swiftly, he pushed some boards aside, revealing a small basement window. He knew exactly where it was; evidently he'd done this before. He wrapped his long coat around himself tightly to keep it out of the way and, feet first, he shinnied through the window and dropped down into the darkness below.

Rachel Mannus scribbled furiously in her notebook, determined to get every word down before any of the doctors caught her and sent her back to bedpan patrol. She was supposed to be mopping floors this morning, not mingling with the patients. But this was a rare opportunity, coming upon all three of them together like this in the shabby patient lounge. Usually, she had to catch up with patients one at a time, whenever she could steal a moment, usually in the wards where there was little or no privacy.

For once, the lounge television set wasn't blaring out soap operas at top volume. Charlie Raymond, a sixty-year-old black man in a wheelchair, was awake and paying attention to the conversation. Terry Saunders, the pretty blond university student who'd gone through the windshield in a nasty auto accident, had recovered enough, even though her head was still bandaged, to participate in the discussion. Roseanne Rizzo, a thirty-two-year-old housewife who'd recently suffered a miscarriage, was telling the little group about her near-death experience while Rachel listened raptly, taking voluminous notes. As she spoke, Roseanne's face seemed to be lit from within; there was no mistaking the sincerity of her words or the authenticity of her experience.

"And suddenly, even though I was in a coma, I saw myself . . . like from above, you know? I was

13

looking down and I saw myself lying there on the bed and everything. . . . Ralph, my husband, was crying. And the doctor was saying that I was dying . . . and I started to float out into the hall and then into this tunnel . . . toward this light, and it was the most beautiful light I ever saw . . ."

"Beautiful light," wrote Rachel into her notebook.

Roseanne's words took on a breathless quality. "And then I heard this voice, and it was the most beautiful voice I ever heard, and it said . . . 'I'm taking your baby, but you are going back.' And then I woke up, and there was Ralph and the doctor. . . ."

Her voice trailed off and the light died out in her face, leaving an ordinary, even rather pathetic woman.

"I was legally dead four and a half minutes," put in the black man, "but I didn't see no tunnel and I didn't see no light—"

"Oh, I did!" Terry interrupted eagerly. "And it was so beautiful!"

"I was in this garden . . ." continued Charlie Raymond, but Terry was on a roll and wouldn't let him talk. Rachel wrote "garden" into her notes.

"And this tunnel . . . and this light . . . and then this . . . like a guide . . . and a chariot . . . and music . . ." she babbled.

Chariot? Music? A guide? Give me a break! Rachel Mannus stopped writing, looked up from her notebook and gave Terry a sharp glance out

14

of her smoky dark eyes under brows as arched and feathery as a moth's antennae. This was too good to be true. She suspected that Terry was embroidering her experience to give Rachel what she thought Rachel wanted to hear.

"I think they'd better get you off medication, Terry," she remarked dryly, but with a sweet smile that took some of the sting out of her words.

"Hsssst . . . hssssst!"

Stuffing her notebook hastily into her lab coat pocket, Rachel looked up. Edna O'Connor, the ward nurse, stood in the doorway with a warning look on her black face. She was jerking her head in the direction of the corridor. Over Edna's shoulder, Rachel could see the doctors approaching on their morning rounds. The nurses had already begun their flurry of activity, so Rachel picked up her mop and was diligently scrubbing away at the floor by the time the doctors arrived with their charts.

"You watch your ass for a while," Edna cautioned under her breath. "They'll be watchin' you kids pretty close. They dumped a third-year student for performing a laparotomy by himself this morning."

Rachel's eyes widened in surprise mingled with alarm. One of her own classmates! "Who?"

The nurse shrugged indifferently. "Labratch . . . or something . . ."

"David Labraccio?" gasped Rachel. Unbelievable, that it should be David. He was such a fantastic student . . . so serious, so dedicated, so hard-working.

"Why are you always talking to the patients about death, anyways?" the nurse asked, curious. Everyone on the ward was curious about this tall, thin, solemn-faced but very attractive young woman with the dark red hair and the thin-rimmed eyeglasses which contrasted so strongly with her wide, sensuous mouth.

Rachel Mannus was like no other medical student the nurses had ever seen. She seemed to be obsessed with death and would listen for as long as she could to any patient who'd "died" or nearly died, and who'd come back from the edge of the grave. There was a lot of speculation in the cafeteria about what the girl's notebooks contained and why.

Without answering, Rachel put her mop back into the bucket. "I'll be late for class," she said quietly. "Thanks, Edna." And she was gone.

Nelson Wright walked up the stairs from the basement and strolled quietly but confidently through the large center hall of the locked building.

At the turn of the century, when Taft had been designed and erected as part of the university's medical college, it had been hailed as one of the monumental beauties of the classical school of Chicago architecture. In the great entrance hall, under the high glass dome of the rotunda, had been painted a series of mighty murals, done in the massive style of Michelangelo, heroic figures with bulging muscles and rippling drapery, depicting great moments in medicine.

Here, in separate panels, were Hippocrates treating the epileptic; Galen holding the spinal cord; Vesalius dissecting a corpse. Here was Harvey lecturing on the circulation of the blood. Edward Jenner and the discovery of immunology. Morton and the first use of ether. Lister and antisepsis. Pasteur and the germ theory of disease. The accomplishments of each of the historical masters of medicine had been immortalized in paint on a vast wall.

High up near the circular ceiling, above the central panel of the mural, was a cast bronze pediment. Inside it was an arresting piece of high-relief sculpture, medieval in feel, at variance with the Graeco-Roman nature of the building itself. The work depicted the struggle between mankind and death. The figure of a man and the figure of a skeleton vied for the possession of a tall winged staff entwined with serpents, standing between the two. The skeleton clutched his scythe, symbol of the Grim Reaper, with one hand, while the other grasped at the caduceus, ancient symbol of the medical profession, the staff that the god Hermes bestowed on Aesculapius. The man's hand also reached for the healing staff, but wasn't quite reaching it.

It was a vivid metaphor in bronze of medicine's eternal struggle to conquer the forces of death, a chilling piece of work that conflicted with the robust wall paintings below it. Looking at the sculpture, the viewer came away with the definite feeling that, try as Man might, he didn't really stand a chance against Death.

Over the years, the murals had darkened and their subjects had been hidden under old varnish and coats of paint. The mosaic floor had cracked and many of the tiles had disappeared, and the gilt had begun to peel off the panelling. The outside walls of the building had suffered decades of erosion caused by extreme midwestern winters and summers and the settling of the bricks. It would be criminal to allow the deterioration of so impressive a structure to continue. Taft was long overdue for a facelift, and was now getting one at last.

Scaffolding had been set up in front of the old paintings, and large plastic dropcloths were laid over the floors. The earliest workers were beginning to show up, taking styrofoam coffee containers and buttery danish out of greasy brown paper bags, lighting cigarettes and cracking jokes. The first coffee break of the day. As Nelson Wright strolled by them, the painters looked startled. Nobody but the renovation crew was supposed to be here. Who the hell—?

Nelson was as surprised to see the workers as they were to see him. They hadn't been here two days ago. Two days ago, Taft had belonged to him. But he didn't lose his cool, and the expensive sunglasses hid his expression.

"Morning. Nice work, very nice," he commented expansively. "You're doing a great job. Keep it up."

Nevertheless, he picked up his pace a bit,

moving quickly past the puzzled workers and into the corridor. The door to the corridor had one of those locks that opened on the inside, but once you were on the other side, the door locked firmly behind you. Opening the door, Nelson took a piece of adhesive tape from under his coat lapel and surreptitiously stuck it over the lock. Now it would open from the outside, too.

CHAPTER 2

David Labraccio's absence from anatomy class didn't pass without notice. The news of his suspension had already swept through the med school like fire through dry grass, fueled by whispers and rumors. He'd popped a surgeon in the eye. He'd done an appendectomy with a spoon, without anesthesia. He'd been caught in the supply closet screwing Duckworth, the gorgon head nurse of the ER. He'd been suspended. He'd been expelled. He'd gone out and gotten drunk. He'd committed suicide. The only fact that everyone agreed on was that Labraccio was bye-bye, a fact that made the other third-year students' blood run cold. To slave like a sonofabitch for so long and then get bounced out on your ass—it was a medical student's nightmare. If it could happen to an honor roll student like David, it could happen to any of them.

Randall Steckle adjusted the volume on his mini tape recorder with one hand as he wielded his scalpel with the other. "I am now beneath the transverse arch of the foot," he told his little Sony, taping his anatomy notes. "The three cuneiforms along with the other two of the metatarsus—" The scalpel traced the path of his words along the left foot of Steckle's assigned cadaver.

"Doctor Steckle, a second opinion, if you'd be so kind." Nelson Wright interrupted him, pointing to the cadaver's right foot, which as Randy's lab partner he'd been assigned to dissect.

The corpses used for dissection lay naked, one to a table, their heads swathed eerily in gauze so that their dead faces could not be seen. Today, only the stomach cavity of each cadaver was exposed, the flesh already opened and peeled back to lay bare the internal organs.

Turning off his recorder, Steckle leaned over the body and took a look at its right foot, which Nelson had been working on. Then he made a slice of his own.

Wright grinned. "Brilliant," he approved. "You be sure to bring all that talent tonight, Doctor."

At the word "tonight," Randy Steckle chewed at his fleshy lower lip and looked distinctly uncomfortable. "Nelson, about tonight—I like you. And because of that, I have to decline on moral grounds. Isn't there enough atrocity in the world without your own little horror?''

Nelson raised one eyebrow, and his pale green eyes glittered. '' 'Horror'?'' he repeated mockingly, drawing the word out for emphasis. ''Steckle, it's ignorance we fear, but since when did 'truth' and 'knowledge' become 'horror' to a scientist . . . and a genius? Especially to a genius like yourself.'' He took another couple of slices at the foot.

When Nelson said ''genius,'' Randy blushed, and his round owlish face looked childishly happy.

''Tic, tac, toe,'' said Nelson Wright wickedly, drawing a line through his three winning crosses, carved with macabre humor on the sole of the body's dead foot. ''You better show.''

Rachel Mannus wasn't happy about sharing a cadaver with Joe Hurley. Although he was a high-ranking student who made excellent grades, as an effective lab partner he left a lot to be desired. Rachel was dedicated to the point of being driven. Medical school was difficult. Her work absorbed all her time and energy, with no time left over for frivolous socializing.

For Joe Hurley, on the other hand, everything came too easily; he wasn't accustomed to working hard and he loved fooling around. Handsome and cocky, with pale skin, jet-black hair and incredibly blue eyes, Joe was a true ''Black Irishman''—mischievous, winning, and a devil with pretty women. In the presence of a woman

23

with a face and body like Rachel's, he couldn't help it; the charm switched on automatically, like a timer that controls house lights when the family's away.

"Good morning, Mannus," he greeted her when she arrived, rather breathless, a minute or two late. "How you doin'?"

"Fine," she muttered. He made her nervous, the way his blue eyes were always raking over her body. Joe Hurley was going to put the moves on her again; she knew it.

"I've been meaning to ask you something. You dating anyone?" he began, as Rachel bent, absorbed, over her side of the cadaver.

The girl gritted her teeth, but as she laid bare the flap of skin all she said was, "Identify."

"Seminal vesicle," answered Hurley easily and correctly, barely giving the body a glance. "It's not offensive if I make conversation, is it? Sometimes it feels good to open up a little. Look at old Lenny there, he's open." He indicated the cadaver between them.

"Identify," said Rachel briefly, again pointing with her scalpel.

"Prostate. You know," Joe continued, his attention more on Rachel than on the anatomy lesson, "I've heard all the rumors and nicknames about you. But I don't believe it." He grinned at her, displaying a dimple in his chin and thirty-two brilliantly white and healthy teeth. "I'm certain that you're really a very warm woman, not in the least bit frigid or repressed." Grabbing the sheet that covered the cadaver, he pulled it down, revealing its naked private parts.

"Identify," he challenged.

"Your brains," snapped Rachel.

The Irish grin widened. "Good. So, you want to come over to my place where we can do some serious thinking?"

"Excuse me, Doctor Hurley." Nelson Wright interrupted them before Rachel could let her anger show. "I need a word with Doctor Mannus." Grabbing her elbow, Nelson pulled Rachel to a quiet place near the window of the anatomy lab.

"Didn't I already say no to this?" demanded Rachel, throwing off his hand, her lovely face darkening with annoyance.

Nelson put one placating hand on her arm. "Look, I already have Hurley and Steckle lined up. Two of the top GPA's in the school."

Rachel shook her head no, attempting to push past him and return to her dissection.

But Nelson Wright was not to be put off so easily. "All I need is for you to handle the injections and the IV."

"Forget it!" scowled Rachel, her voice cold. The whole damn thing repelled her utterly. Of all the half-assed ideas she'd ever encountered, Wright's was by far the most ill-conceived. She wanted no part of it.

There was a small commotion at the front of the anatomy lab as Professor Zho bustled in importantly, followed by two teaching assistants carrying the dreaded blue examination booklets. This was a crucial two-part exam: a written, followed by an oral, as the cadavers were dissected under Zho's implacable Oriental gaze.

"Good morning, class. Today's exam will be scaled," she said without preamble. "Three A's will be given, five B's, ten C's and the remaining four will get D's and F's."

A unanimous groan rose from the class, then it occurred suddenly to half the students in the room that Labraccio's suspension would free up one of the A grades, and give everybody a better chance, and a feeling of guilty gratitude swept the laboratory.

Rachel started back to her lab table, but Nelson pulled at her sleeve. "I'm also working on a special mystery guest," he said softly, only for her ears. "A future surgical 'Hall of Famer' . . ."

Despite herself, Rachel was interested. "Who's that?" she whispered back. "Powell? Westheimer?"

But Nelson only put one finger to his lips and shook his head. "Show up and you'll see."

"Once again, as in life," continued the anatomy professor, "you are not in competition with me, yourself, or this exam, but with each other."

Rachel shook her head firmly. "Sorry, Nelson, I have no interest in watching you kill yourself."

A sly smile crept across the boy's features, and his green eyes shone strangely. "I think you do," he said softly. "Wouldn't it be easier than snooping around the hospital for all that *National Enquirer* 'back from the dead' crap?"

The girl's eyes widened in surprise and she turned to stare at him. How on earth could he know?

"Mister Wright?" called Dr. Zho. "Are you planning to participate?"

Nelson flashed a brilliant smile, first at the teacher and then at Rachel, a smile that told her he'd delivered his coup.

"Absolutely," he said.

"The entire plan is not only arrogant, but risky as hell," Randall Steckle pointed out as he scrubbed the last of the blood and tissue from under his fingernails.

"I'm in perfect health; it's a controlled situation. No blood loss. Minimal risk," countered Nelson Wright from the next sink. Nelson, Randy Steckle and Hurley were washing up in the men's room after the exam. "Come on, you two are the guys who brought that dog back after it was dead for almost four hours."

"We were lucky," Hurley protested. "The dog had frozen to death. Greyhounds have very strong hearts."

"And the dog was smarter than you," Steckle put in.

"Nine o'clock at the old Dog Lab, Taft. Are you gonna be there?" Nelson challenged.

"Of course not," said Joe.

"Thank God," Steckle murmured fervently.

But Nelson merely gave one of his trademark cool shrugs. "Look, there are others in this school who'd like to make a name for them-

27

selves out of something like this. It just seems a shame to me that people with ability don't have the nerve."

Hurley balled up his paper towel and threw it to the floor. "All right!" he declared, challenged. "You want it, you got it. I'm a very busy man, but we'll be there."

We? Where did Hurley get "we"? It was one thing to talk about it—medical students were always fantasizing about some mad doctor experiment or another—but it was an entirely other thing to actually make a plan to carry one of the dumb ideas out. Randall Steckle's mouth opened in protest, but all that came out was a feeble squeak. "Speak for yourself."

"Sure, it'll be dramatic," sneered Joe. "You'll cry, you'll faint, at best you'll puke, but then what? 'Cause frankly, Nelson, I don't think you have the balls."

Nelson Wright smiled. They knew that smile, too wide and too bright, a little crazy even. "You bring your equipment, gentlemen. I'll bring the balls."

After he stormed out of the hospital, David Labraccio did what he always did when he was angry or frustrated or both: he did something intensely physical.

What Labraccio really wanted now was a mountain to climb. He wanted the feel of crampons on his boots, pitons in one hand and his pickaxe in the other. He wanted the smell of a mountain close to his face as he swung from his nylon rope, looking for toeholds. A clean smell, the smell of ancient stone, of reassuring massive and unchanging power. He longed for the huge expenditure of energy that marked the ascent, and the wonderful feeling of triumph when he reached the top and stood alone, breathing the thin purity of icy mountain air, surveying the vista spread beneath him, knowing that he'd conquered once again. Just David versus the Goliath of the mountain.

But where the hell do you find a mountain in the flat prairie land of America's middle west? So instead, he shot baskets. He walked all the way home, clear to the other side of the city, while rage and humiliation fought to overmaster him. Storming into his apartment, crowded with textbooks and athletic equipment, David grabbed up his high school basketball and ran out into the concrete backyard of his building, where he'd set up a makeshift hoop.

For hours he played alone, pushing his body to the brink of exhaustion, racing around the court as though the Lakers were hell-for-leather after him, making two- and three-point shots from every angle. Fit and coordinated, David often expressed his emotions—or perhaps repressed his emotions—in sheer physical activity. All his life, he'd been a jock as well as a brain, captaining his high school teams, attending college on two scholarships, one scholastic, one athletic. Now in medical school where there were no teams, he had to play sports by himself. But that's why he loved mountain climbing—it was

29

a solitary achievement.

At last, dripping with sweat, trembling in his knees and calves, his shoulders aching, Labraccio went inside to shower and to pack. He was going home. What else was there to do? Faced with confronting his father and mother and telling them the painful truth—that he'd been canned from med school—David acted characteristically. He wouldn't postpone the pain or avoid it by telephoning. He'd drive back home and tell them himself, face to face. Then, he supposed, he'd get a job at the Seven-Eleven. As for ever coming back here . . . forget it. No way.

Labraccio had packed his canvas-covered army surplus truck with all his sports equipment—bat, balls, hockey stick, pickaxe and other climbing gear, lacrosse net, racquets —and was throwing his bulging backpack out the window to the street, so he wouldn't have to carry it, when Nelson Wright's sardonic face appeared around the back wall of the building.

"Yo, Labraish, where you off to?"

Angrily, David slung his legs over the third-floor window frame and rappelled down the side of the building on his climbing rope. He picked himself up and hurled his bags into the truck. "I'm outta here. Don't stand between me and the road."

"Look, so they slapped you with a temporary suspension. It's only four months. It won't even affect your scholarship."

Labraccio shook his head, his mouth a thin

line. "It doesn't matter. I'm through with medicine."

"You're the best student this school's ever had," argued Nelson, meaning it. "They don't let guys like you walk away from medicine. Besides, you were wrong."

David Labraccio whipped around, facing his friend. His face was a mask of anguish. "My God, she was dying!" he cried. "I saved her life! What the hell would you have done?"

"Why are you taking this so personally?" Wright shrugged, dodging the question. "Of course they're gonna make an example of you to protect their insurance bond. They'll ask you back next term."

Labraccio shook his head; plainly, Nelson had no idea what he was talking about, or what the basic issues were here. "It doesn't matter," he said dully. "Given the same situation, I'd do it again."

"I know you would." Nelson Wright smiled. "That's why I need you there tonight."

But David had turned away again, and was moving his sports equipment around to make more room for the rest of his stuff in the truck. "There are a few people I'd like to kill right now, however you're not one of them."

"Hey, I don't want to die," said Nelson quickly, and that febrile smile lit up his face again. "I want to come back with the answers to death and life. I can get there with the others, but I need you to bring me back. I need you," he said again.

Labraccio shook his head again. "Sorry, I can't do it," was all he said.

Nelson Wright felt desperation beginning to claw at his insides, but he fought back the panic and kept his voice light and level. David Labraccio was his ace in the hole, the "mystery guest" he'd hinted at to Rachel. The success of his plan hinged vitally on the skill of the students who would resuscitate him; they were all amateurs, but some were less amateur than others. Labraccio was the best available.

"Okay," he said brusquely. "Man, why don't you just walk away? Go climb a mountain. Today you burned your career for a stranger, and now you're turning your back on a friend." A low blow, but Nelson knew it was a strategic one. Now he let a note of empathy creep into his voice. "Hey, I'm really sorry about what happened. But what are my chances of making it back without you?"

"Then don't do it," said David in a low tone.

Nelson Wright's smile broke forth in all its phosphorescent glory. "But what if it works?" he whispered. "What if it really works?"

Rachel Mannus's mood, always serious, tonight was somber. As she moved around the wards, doing the menial tasks to which medical students are assigned—emptying bedpans, mopping floors, changing bedlinen—her thoughts were not on her chores. She was thinking about Nelson Wright and his bizarre idea.

Was he serious? Did he actually intend to

carry out this deranged plan to push the envelope of death, to allow himself to die under controlled conditions in order to explore the near-death experience? What if the resuscitation didn't work? Didn't he know he was really laying his life on the line? Didn't he care?

There was risk and there was risk. What David Labraccio did, risking his med school standing to save a human life, that was understandable. Rachel felt sorry for David, she respected him and in her shy, quiet way she liked and admired him. But what Nelson Wright had proposed, had pushed and bullied and teased her toward, that was incomprehensible to Rachel. In that direction madness lay. To actually experience clinical death—heart death, brain death—and to attempt to come back from it with information, as though you'd been away on vacation and were bringing back color slides—no, unthinkable!

If such an experiment was possible, why hadn't it been performed before, under ideal conditions, by well-trained laboratory scientists? Perhaps prisoners serving life sentences, or terminal patients, would volunteer for it. Surely death, not space, was the last great frontier. To a doctor, death was the greatest enemy of all, so far the undefeated enemy. The mortality rate is always one hundred percent. One person, one death. Two people, two deaths.

Oh, but the temptation to make the experiment was insidious, and Nelson knew it. He was like the snake in the Garden of Eden, holding out the fruit of the Tree of Knowledge, murmuring

"Take a bite," while his green eyes glittered like eager emeralds. And he knew his customers, all right.

Who better than med students, young, strong, immortal, to test their newly-fledged powers on the oldest enemy? They didn't even have to go themselves. Nelson had volunteered. Nelson was the only guinea pig going. What if he *did* come back? What if he brought back with him knowledge that nobody had ever had before? Knowledge that could help humankind overcome death?

"I'm going to die, aren't I?" Mrs. Ashby put one feeble hand on Rachel's arm as the girl straightened her bedclothes and patted down her pillows.

Startled out of her thoughts, Rachel looked down at the old woman in the ward bed. No, not so old. Elizabeth Ashby was no more than sixty-five, but so ravaged by her ovarian cancer that she appeared to be eighty. She was a terminal case; it was only a matter of weeks, days perhaps, and both of them knew it, but one of them was afraid to accept it, and the other colluded in the lie.

"No . . . no, of course not . . ." stammered Rachel, and gave her a tentative, sympathetic smile, turning away from the fear in the woman's haggard face.

A smile was so little to give! But what if she had more? What if she could possess the knowledge that came from the other side of the grave, as a surety to offer as comfort to the dying? What

34

if Nelson Wright could give them all that little bit more to offer where it was needed? Rachel Mannus's thoughts were in turmoil.

Joe Hurley was doing his homework. How he loved doing his homework. He studied all his subjects with equal enthusiasm. Blondes, brunettes, redheads. Irish girls, Jewish girls, Italian girls, black girls, Asian girls. Girls with large warm breasts, and girls with itty-bitty titties. Divine Providence had given Joe a pair of killer blue eyes, a handsome face, a live-wire body and an overactive libido. Who was Joe Hurley to fly in the face of the Almighty's obvious intentions? Joe was born to get laid, and he strove always to fulfill that destiny.

This afternoon Joe's homework was a pintsized doll, a campus waitress named Bridget, piquant and sexy in her little starched apron. Hurley had chatted her up over endless refills of coffee, and it didn't take a lot of doing to lure her up to his messy loft when her shift ended for the evening. In that loft they were presently thrashing around in his waterbed, making the beast with two backs. Just the two of them, and, oh yes, Joe's state-of-the-art video camcorder, which was busily recording the action from its strategic hiding place on Joe's closet shelf, opposite the bed.

As usual, Hurley had switched his answering machine on, so when the phone rang, the machine would pick up the call.

"Leave a message after the beep." Joe

Hurley's answering machine humor was rather like Joe himself: cut-to-the-chase.

"Hi, honey." Anne's voice came sweetly through the telephone. "I just went to the printers and Mom picked out our invitations. It's going to be such a beautiful wedding. Call me. I miss you. I love you." Click.

As his fiancée left her message, Joe didn't miss a beat, but kept putting the blocks to Bridget in an escalating rhythm. Anne didn't have anything to do with this. Anne he loved; Anne was serious business, a lifetime commitment. But fucking pretty girls was Joe's hobby, and every man ought to have a hobby. Especially one at which he was very, very good.

"Who was that?" gasped Bridget between moans and miaows.

"My sister," gasped Joe cheerfully.

"You're going to marry your sister?" Even Bridget wasn't quite that gullible, but when Hurley began nibbling on her neck she subsided once more into passionate whimpers.

The phone rang again, and Nelson Wright's deep voice came through the answering machine after the beep.

"I know you're there, 'Doctor' Hurley. Don't be late and bring your camera." Click.

"Camera?" asked Bridget with a sudden thrill of fear. "What camera?"

Rachel Mannus moved quietly through the ward, stopping to straighten a bed for one patient, pour a drink of water for another, all small menial tasks that medical students were assigned to do to take some of the burden off the overworked nursing staff. The patients all liked the girl; she was never brusque or impatient with them, and she possessed a gentleness and empathy that warmed them whenever they saw her.

Now she stopped again for a moment by the bedside of Mrs. Ashby, her terminal cancer patient, whose skin was stretched thin as paper over her painful bones.

The woman's hand came up to grip Rachel's with a strength that was surprising in one of her frailty.

"Don't let them bury me on a Saturday," she pleaded, her eyes begging. "It costs fifty dollars more to be buried on a Saturday."

Rachel bit her lip. This was so painful to watch, a woman dying with only her family's lack of money on her mind to torture her. "You're doing much better," she lied, pressing the woman's hand where it clung tightly to her own.

If only there were something that she could do to help!

Nelson Wright sat alone in his apartment, as he did almost every evening, as he'd sat alone for so much of his life. Only this night was different. This night would be the culmination of a dream, a dream forged years ago, when he was twelve, and refined over the years from a dream to a scheme and then to a plan.

Tonight the plan would be put into effect.

Nelson's ferocious intelligence had gone over it a thousand times, digging for flaws, finding none. The only real risks, the only unknown variables, lay in the others—the ones who would send him there and bring him back. That is, if everything went according to plan.

If it had been possible, Nelson wouldn't have allowed any others into the plan. If he could have relied only on himself, he would have done so. But it wasn't possible. He couldn't do it alone; he couldn't make himself die under hospital conditions and resuscitate himself on schedule. He couldn't make a living record of the proceedings. Little as he liked it, he needed the help of others.

So he'd done the next best thing; he'd hand-picked his doubting, reluctant associates. From a class of one hundred and seventy medical students, he'd chosen four to make the experiment with, four—he hoped—of the best.

David Labraccio. The top student of the third-year class. The fastest set of responses. The most accomplished technician. But his flaw was a moral and ethical squeamishness unnecessary to the plan.

Joe Hurley. Smart and unscrupulous enough to stay cold under pressure. After all, it wasn't his ass on the line, but Nelson's. His flaw: a lack of commitment to anything or anybody. Would he go the distance?

Randall Steckle. A genius, at least theoretically. An encyclopedic textbook knowledge combined with an inquiring mind. Steckle and Hurley went way back together, to grade school. Where Hurley led, Steckle would probably follow. But how far? Nelson needed Randy, because he had to have a definitive record of the experiment. Steckle had a way with words; he was tape-recording his own medical school career, turning it into a book. Between Steckle's little Sony recorder and Joe's camcorder, the experiment would be properly documented. But Randy's flaw was that he was, after all, a kid, only twenty-four where the others were twenty-six, and besides, he was something of a pussy and a dweeb. Faced with a crisis, he might easily crack.

Rachel Mannus. There was the mystery. She was capable, clever, intelligent and curious, hungry for knowledge. Also, she had this strange fascination with death, especially the near-death experience. You'd think that she'd be the first to say yes to an experiment like his. Yet she was the most reluctant of them all, and Nelson still didn't know whether he'd persuaded her to join them. And her weaknesses? Another mystery. Nelson had to admit to himself that he had no idea at all what they could turn out to be. But if Rachel showed up at the Dog Lab tonight, he might find out.

Nelson's apartment was huge, bare and stark,

with high ceilings, empty white walls and a minimum of furniture. Of all things, he preferred silence and high, vast, empty spaces. He owned an antique Victorian desk of great value, on which sat a PC much better than the one he'd asked those unanswerable questions, half a lifetime ago. It still didn't answer the unanswerable, though.

Now, only an hour or so away from his appointed destiny in the Dog Lab, Nelson Wright turned to the keyboard again, tapping out a document—a release from responsibility for his companions in the experiment. His fingers shook a little on the keys as he typed it, and he kept making mistakes.

". . . absolving all participants from this voluntary act." He finished at last, and hit the PRINT button. The printer began to chatter as the letter was commited to paper.

Standing up, Nelson walked into his bathroom, a room as antiseptic and white as the rest of the apartment. Running water into the marble sink, he splashed water on his face. In the bathroom mirror, his reflection looked already dead. His face was deathly pale, and dark rings circled his eyes, which seemed to him to be lighter than usual, flat yet fathomless.

No. He would not allow fear to control him. This experiment was his idea, his own decision, something he'd planned for a long time. It was risky, sure, but the rewards were incalculable. And life without those rewards was not something Nelson wanted to consider.

The printer had stopped; the apartment was silent. Nelson pulled the letter from the roller and read it through. Then, with a shaky hand which he had to steady, he signed it. Now he was ready.

Nelson Wright was going to have a look-see.

CHAPTER 3

The Taft building was deserted for the night; all the workers had gone home long ago, leaving draped scaffolding that resembled huge mysterious shrouded figures. Heavy sheets of plastic hung from the ceilings like weird draperies, protecting the woodwork from plaster dust and asbestos. The smell of paint thinner and other solvents permeated the narrow hallway that led from the central rotunda to the labs.

Randall Steckle wrinkled his nose uneasily. This place was really creepy. He hated all this—an empty old building, strange forms in the semidarkness, a silence broken only by his footsteps and the rolling casters on his dolly, the chemical fumes irritating his sinuses. Anxiously, he pushed the large canister of nitrous oxide down the corridor, resisting the impulse to look behind him every five seconds. Above all he hated the secrecy, the creeping around in the dark, afraid of every little noise. This whole damn experiment was just too damn spooky. Trust Nelson to locate a ghost town like this for his crazy games.

The sudden, loud sound, a squeaking of large wheels coming from God-knows-where, unnerved Randy completely. He froze. There was something out there—something large and white, rolling toward him out of the eerie darkness. He ducked down, out of sight. Should he run? No, shit. It was only a gurney, and Joe Hurley was pushing it. Over Joe's shoulder was slung his camcorder.

Steckle showed his teeth in a relieved grin. "Ah, the bed," he cracked. "Thank God he called a specialist."

"No lectures, Steckle."

But Randy had found a sore spot, and he went on digging into it. "Why should I expect," he asked Joe rhetorically, "that after you became engaged you just might grow up?"

Side by side the two old friends moved slowly down the corridor, wheeling their assigned burdens. Hurley looked aggrieved at Steckle's remarks. "Did it ever dawn on you that I'm working some things out . . . recording some last adventures so I can resign myself to monogamy with the perfect woman?" he retorted defensively.

"No, it never dawned on me for a moment. But the words 'pussy marauder' did occasionally pop into mind."

They reached the door that Nelson Wright had taped. It opened easily. They held it for each other until the gurney and the nitrous had been wheeled safely through. The Dog Lab was only a few doors down.

Abandoned for months, the vast Dog Lab had a stale, musty odor, reminiscent of uncleaned animal cages. It was freezing cold in there, and both Randy and Joe suppressed small shivers. Also, the large room was very dark. Anything could be hiding in the shadows of the far corners near the walls. Roaches, rats, maybe even something a lot worse.

"What the hell are we doing?" Steckle burst out. "This is good-bye med school, good-bye career—"

"Chill out, 'Testickle,'" said Joe, invoking Randy's grammar school nickname. "Ten bucks says he won't do it. Shits his drawers and we're outta here. Twenty bucks he doesn't even show."

Randy reached for the light switch on the wall. Out of the shadows a strange hand closed over his own, preventing him from turning on the lights. Steckle squeaked, nearly jumping out of his skin.

"No lights." Nelson Wright's voice was husky in the darkness. "Security will come running." There was a click, and Randy blinked as two sudden bright spots of light blinded him momentarily. Nelson had pulled the shades down and switched on a pair of high-beam emergency work lights. "Set it up over the grate," he instructed. "I just got the boiler going."

Joe Hurley's black eyebrows shot up in amazement when he saw the setup waiting for them. Nelson had put together a complete resuscitation unit, almost as good as the one in the hospital ER. There were EEG and EKG monitors, an IV stand, defib paddles and an electrical charger—just about everything they'd need. There was even one of those rolling crash carts from the ER, to hold the syringes and the medications they'd need. It must have taken him weeks to assemble all of this stuff out of the different labs in Taft, and get it up and running.

"You're not really going to do this," Steckle started to protest. All evening, he'd been having not only second thoughts, but third and fourth thoughts as well, and they all said, you guys are stone crazy.

"Shut up, Steckle," Nelson growled.

"Just humor the man," Hurley said sarcastically to Steckle. But the two of them obeyed, cowed by Nelson's determination and his air of authority. They moved the gurney to the spot that Nelson chose, where it was already starting to get a little warmer, and set up the canister of nitrous oxide at its side, ready for use.

Without further preliminaries, Nelson Wright began to strip off his shirt and sweater, revealing a thin body with a prominent ribcage and square bony shoulders. When he was down to his trousers and his socks, he stopped.

"You'll take me down with nitrous, sodium pentothal, and the refrigerated blanket," he instructed briskly and without emotion. "When my body temperature reaches eighty-six degrees, hit me once with two hundred joules to stop the heart. When it does, my heart is dead. Take off the mask."

Pulling himself up on the gurney, Nelson Wright began to connect to his head the eight EEG leads that were attached to the electroencephalographic monitor that would record his brain activity. When they were attached by means of suction cups to his forehead, temple and cranium, he lay down. Whatever he might be feeling inside, he didn't let it show, but an animal would have detected the fear oozing from his pores.

Randy and Joe stood frozen, unwilling and unable to believe that Nelson was going through with this insane experiment. He was actually getting ready to die, to go under and stop breathing, become brain-dead and heart-dead for one full minute, sixty interminable seconds. This was true madness.

"Cups, Doctor Hurley," called Nelson impatiently, and Joe was startled into action. He took the EKG electrodes, which led from the electrocardiograph that would monitor Nelson's heartbeat, and pressed the suction cups to Wright's arms, legs and heart.

"Where's Mannus?" croaked Steckle through

trembling lips. "You said Rachel was coming."

Nelson didn't bother to reply to the question. The truth was, he had no idea whether Rachel Mannus would show or not. He went on issuing his instructions.

"I'm gonna draw twenty cc's of sodium pentothal. Steckle, you handle the injections. Once the EEG flatlines and the brain is dead, I'll be exploring. At thirty seconds, flick the blanket to the 'warm' setting and bring me up to ninety-three degrees. Slowly. Inject one cc of adrenaline. Joe moves in at one minute with the defibrillator paddles and I come back to life."

"With brain damage," said Rachel from the door of the lab. "In many ways resembling a Cabbage Patch kid."

"Not with a body temp of eighty-six degrees," smiled Nelson. "Doctor Mannus, will you handle the injections?"

Rachel hesitated, scanning Nelson's face as though trying to read his thoughts. He looked back at her without blinking, letting her see his determination. At last, she nodded.

"Wait a minute—" called Randall Steckle. "Wait. Quite simply, why are you doing this?"

"Quite simply, to see if there's anything out there, beyond death," replied Nelson. "For the first time in history, man has the technology to see it all. Philosophy failed. Religion failed. And now it's up to us . . . the physical sciences. I think mankind deserves to know."

"So, you're doing this for 'mankind'?" Joe

Hurley cocked a cynical eyebrow.

"This is not for mankind, this is for Nelson," Steckle said hotly. "Why do I see him squeezed between Andy Rooney and the new Subaru commercial? 'Tonight on *60 Minutes*, a brilliant young medical student who dared to experience death and lived to talk about it.'"

Nelson Wright smiled his private smile. "Fame, of course, will be inevitable."

"That's the wrong reason," said Rachel quietly.

"But it's the right idea. Here—" Nelson put his hand into his trousers pocket and pulled out the letter, handing it to Joe. "This absolves you guys from any blame . . . just in case."

"Nelson—" said Randy feebly.

"How about a little of that nitrous, Rachel?" interrupted Nelson. "At least I'll be going out with a laugh. Hurley, get the blanket. We're all professionals, and, ah, I'm sure everything will go smoothly."

"Nelson, if you die, can I have your apartment?"

Rachel gasped, and both she and the astonished Randy Steckle turned to glare at Hurley.

"A joke, just a joke," shrugged Joe, but even he was embarrassed.

"One minute," said Nelson. "Dead for one minute, then back again. Don't be late. Start filming, Director Hurley."

Shouldering his camcorder, Joe began shooting the gurney with its passenger into the unknown. Reaching down, Nelson clicked the stiff refrigerated water blanket—made of space-age material with refrigerant coils and heating coils on separate control systems—on to its coldest setting. To the others, he appeared to be calm and totally without fear.

Steckle, on the other hand, was trembling visibly as he gave Nelson the nitrous oxide mask. Rachel bent over Nelson and slipped the intravenous needle into his arm, then, with one decisive thrust, she shoved the sodium pentothal cartridge into the IV.

Nelson looked Rachel straight in the face. "Promise me you'll go through with this," he whispered urgently.

"I'll see you soon," the girl whispered back.

He raised the nitrous oxide mask to his face and put it over his mouth and nose. Then he raised his right thumb in a salute, and started on his journey into death.

The three others stood staring at him as he slipped into unconsciousness, almost unwilling to believe that he was going through with it. The monitors, EEG and EKG, kept feeding out Nelson's vital signs, in the form of two sets of parallel lines transcribed by two sets of needles made visible on twin screens. Paper printouts from the monitors unrolled as a permanent record, each peak and valley on them a significant reading of Nelson's vital signs.

Rachel Mannus was the first one to come back to attention. She checked the gauge on the refrigerated blanket, and placed an oxygen mask over Nelson's face. The experiment called for his being supplied with oxygen until he was clinically dead. Then, the cutoff, to ensure brain death as well.

"Ninety-six degrees," she announced.

"Please, let him sleep it off," Steckle said nervously. His round cherubic face looked like a crying baby's, and he was beginning to sweat, even in the icy coldness of the lab. "He'll have a wet dream and think it was heaven."

"Good idea," seconded Hurley.

"Ninety-four degrees," said Rachel, not taking her eyes off the temperature reading.

"It's only for a minute," said Joe Hurley. "We have his letter."

"That letter means shit!" yelped Randy. He was really scared now. This was deeper water than he'd ever treaded in his trouble-free life.

"Well, now I know why I'm here," Rachel told them coldly. "He must have known you two would bail out." She snatched up the charged defibrillator paddles and rubbed them together to increase the charge. "Two hundred joules, standing by."

Steckle headed for the door. "I think I've expressed myself clearly for the record. Good night."

"Steckle's probably right," said Joe, nervously wetting his lips. "Are you willing to risk everything, your career, your future, for Nelson's fame?"

51

Rachel hesitated. She checked the monitors. The EKG lines had slowed down, but the transcribing needles were still making shallow peaks and valleys. It wasn't too late. Nelson Wright wasn't dead yet. They could still stop this entire business and everybody could go home and forget all about it. Reason and sanity dictated just that.

Suddenly, Randy Steckle came charging back. "Someone's coming!" he said hoarsely in a terrified whisper.

"Get rid of them!" Rachel snapped.

"Oh, shit!" breathed Joe. They were in the crapper now. There was nothing they could do, with Nelson lying there under that damn blanket, his temperature, pulse, respiration, and brain function continuing to slow down, heading farther into death by the second. They couldn't leave him. They'd be caught in the act and all of them would be expelled.

The footsteps came closer. The three of them held their breath.

Somebody came through the door of the Dog Lab. It was David Labraccio.

"Is he dead?" asked David, looking at Nelson, who lay unmoving under the blanket with his eyes closed.

"He's only sleeping," Joe Hurley said softly.

"Thank God you're here!" Randall Steckle burst out. "Talk some sense into these people!"

Looking around at all of them, Labraccio grasped the situation at once. They'd changed

52

their minds; they were going to bring Nelson back before he croaked; the experiment would be a wipeout. He owed Nelson Wright more than this. David Labraccio stepped up to Rachel. "I'll do it," he told her, holding his hand out for the defibrillator paddles.

"You taking over?" Rachel Mannus flashed him a resentful look.

"I have nothing to lose," David reminded her gently.

"Just his life," Steckle said.

Months ago, Nelson Wright had thought the whole experiment out carefully. "You'll bring me down with nitrous, sodium pentothal, and the refrigerated blanket," he'd ordered. "At eighty-six degrees, hit me once with two hundred joules to stop the heart. When it stops, take off the mask."

The temperature gauge on the blanket read eighty-eight degrees. If they were going to do it, it had to be soon. If they were going to bring him back before he died, it had to be now. Every second lost could prove fatal.

"I can get him back." David Labraccio sounded quietly confident. Again, he held his hand out to Rachel; this time she gave him the charged defib paddles. He was going to carry out Nelson's plan.

"Don't think I couldn't have." She was miffed, and for good reason. She felt that Labraccio was questioning her abilities. "Eighty-six degrees."

Taking the paddles, David called "Clear," and

put them down hard on Nelson's chest, sending two hundred joules of electricity into Nelson Wright's body. The body convulsed, bucking into the air. The heart stopped. Labraccio reached for the oxygen mask.

"No!" yelled Steckle in panic.

"What the fuck?" Joe Hurley moved forward quickly, grabbing hold of Labraccio's arm, but David shoved him away angrily, pulling the mask off Nelson's face.

"Asshole!" he spat at Joe.

"You're killing him! It's murder!" yelled Steckle, on the verge of hysteria. "No wonder you got tossed!"

"This is not the type of shit I want on my transcript," muttered Hurley.

Suddenly, there was a loud beep, and everybody gasped. The beep was followed by a steady, high-pitched drone. All four of them fixed their gaze on the EKG monitor. The peaks and valleys had disappeared, replaced by a long, steady, flat line running across the monitor screen.

"Flatline," Rachel Mannus said quietly.

They all knew what that meant. Clinical death. No vital signs. Nelson had no pulse, no heartbeat, no respiration. Just . . . flatline.

"Keep filming," Labraccio ordered harshly. All his attention was focused now on the still form of Nelson Wright, a body without oxygen.

"Please don't!" cried Steckle, who had now totally lost it. "Don't do anymore! I didn't come to med school to murder my classmates, no matter how deranged they might be!"

"Quiet!" barked Rachel, standing on the other side of the gurney. She, too, could think of nothing but Nelson. Her actions complemented David's, as though they'd always worked together.

David Labraccio had removed the oxygen mask from Nelson's face. Now Rachel Mannus switched off the EKG. They waited in silence, everyone staring at the EEG monitor, on which the wave patterns made by the seven needles were becoming shallower and shallower, while the printout unwound from the machine in a long ribbon of paper on which Nelson Wright's brain function, deprived of vital oxygen, was reduced to nothing more than a squiggly line.

"I wonder what he's thinking," breathed Joe softly.

"The heart has stopped," said Labraccio with scientific objectivity. "Oxygen is running out. Could be panic."

"Or pleasant resolve," offered Rachel.

Shallower and shallower. Shallower and shallower. The parallel lines were flattening out, as before their eyes Nelson Wright's brain was dying from lack of oxygen. Soon the lines would be entirely flat, seven deadly flat lines. And Nelson would be dead.

"He's dipping," whispered Randy Steckle, his eyes round and owlish behind his thick glasses.

After an eternity which took only seconds, the monitor beeped loudly once, then began to drone. The lines went flat at last. Labraccio reached over and switched the monitor sound off. Steckle groaned and dropped his head into his hands. He was dreadfully afraid, as were they all. They'd all been a party here to something unknown.

"Brain death. Now it's real," said Rachel Mannus without emotion. Her facial expression was unreadable, her thoughts far away, trying to follow Nelson Wright into his near-death experience.

"Turn it back on." Steckle's voice was barely audible. "It's too quiet."

Nodding, David Labraccio switched the EEG monitor back on. The machine's drone filled the room.

"Let me defib him," Steckle begged. He was close to tears. "He's dead. That's enough. Let me try to bring him back."

"Watch the door," David ordered curtly. "If we get caught, we're all dead."

"Excuse me," whispered Hurley nervously. "I don't want to ruin anyone's evening, but are we in a room with a dead man?"

None of the others paid attention to him. Rachel glanced at her watch, a large, clear face with a sweep second hand. She made a note of the precise time.

"One minute to go," she said, her eyes on the second hand moving inexorably around the dial, carrying Nelson's fate with it. "Keep filming."

The only sounds in the room were the drone

56

of the monitor signal and a small whirring noise from Joe's camcorder. In silence now they could only watch and wait, they in their own void, Nelson Wright in his.

CHAPTER 4

In all the years that he'd pictured an experimental journey into death, Nelson Wright had never imagined anything exactly like this.

Just as Rachel did, Nelson had lapped up all the stories of those who'd come back from the beyond—the patients who'd "died" on the operating table; men and women who'd been shot, or had drowned, or had met some other violent end only to be snatched back into life by modern technology, or quick-thinking paramedics, or by what the tabloid newspapers described as a "miracle." He'd read their narrations of their own journeys into uncharted death.

Almost all their accounts of near-death experience had contained remarkable similarities. Almost all of them had spoken of two things: a tunnel they passed through which led them up to a light, effulgent, irresistible. The light drew them into the heart of itself. The second corresponding element was that they'd been disembodied, able to "float above" and "look down" at their own bodies lying dead below. So Nelson had incorporated those three images—tunnel, light and disembodiment—into his frequent mental projections of his own experimental dying.

When he flatlined, the first thing Nelson noticed was that, while he did see light, it was very different from what was reported by others who had been there and come back. There was no actual tunnel filled with heavenly light. Instead, it was much more like the bright sunshine of a summer's day. Surrounding, suffusing, bathing Nelson in its radiance, the brilliant daylight pulled him forward, making him run into the heart of it. And Nelson went willingly, happily, like a baby to its mother, for love and warmth and sustenance. He was like a child again; he could hear childish voices somewhere.

But the second element was missing; he didn't feel disembodied. Nelson didn't find himself floating above the gurney and looking down on his dead body below. Quite the contrary, he'd never felt so physically alive. He was aware of his fingers and toes, experiencing and relishing the "fiveness" of them. He could actually feel the blood coursing through his veins, even though his heart had stopped. His thick, dark-blond hair lifted on his scalp and blew lazily in a summer breeze and he was aware of every individual hair. His skin, the largest organ of the body, felt supersensitive, as though drinking in sensations and thirsting for more.

It crossed Nelson's mind briefly that death was not unlike the ultimate acid trip, but before he could even finish forming the thought, he found himself deeply involved in the beautiful summer day.

There was grass, springy and fresh under his feet as he ran happily across it, mashing the dandelions under his sneakers, laughing at the puffball release of the white seed-clouds from the crushed flowertops. From the field nearby he could smell the ripe wheat; the full-grown stalks shimmered in the sunlight and waved their fertile heads, heavy with grain.

Nelson heard the sound of a young dog joyously barking, and of other voices, boys' voices, and he knew suddenly and with certainty that he, too, was a boy again. How old? Eight? Nine? He wasn't sure, but he somehow thought nine. He only knew for certain that it was high summer, that school was out, he was playing, he had friends, he was happy.

"Thirty seconds to go," said David Labraccio. "Okay, here we go. Let's heat him up." He clicked the refrigerated blanket onto the "warm" setting, and the activated heating coils began to glow red.

* * *

It was tag they were playing—racing now over the meadow, and Nelson was "It." He chased after the other boys, looking to tag somebody else, to make another boy "It," but as fast as he ran they ran faster. He was completely aware of his legs moving, of the calf muscles flexing under the blue denim of his jeans, of his living heart pumping blood. It was so beautiful, so very, very beautiful. Why hadn't he gone back sooner?

Labraccio checked the body temperature; it was rising, definitely rising. "Temperature at eighty-nine, ninety. Twenty seconds to go," he alerted them. "At ninety-one stand by with sodium bicarb and eppy. Rachel, charge the paddles."

Randy Steckle reached for the syringes of epinephrine and sodium bicarbonate that were ready on the crash cart, but Rachel called out, "Wait, Steckle, not yet. Temp at ninety-two." They continued to wait, on the alert for Nelson's bodily changes. Now they were functioning as a team.

Round and round his feet ran the dog, now staying close, now bounding away, his tongue out and panting, his tail wagging with excitement. The game became more challenging. Nelson had been "It" for a long time, but the other boys continued to elude him, dodging just out of his reach. Everybody was laughing. The sun was

hot on the back of Nelson's neck; he could feel
the beginnings of a sunburn. It was a white
sun . . . terribly, terribly white . . . and it
seemed to be growing bigger in the sky . . .
bigger and hotter . . . and closer . . .

"Body temp at ninety-three," called Randall
Steckle.

David Labraccio grabbed the charged
defibrillator paddles from Rachel. He yelled
"Clear!" and slammed them against Nelson
Wright's naked torso. Two hundred joules of
current raced through Nelson's body, sending it
into a violent convulsion, lifting it in the air
above the gurney.

It fell back, lifeless.

"Nothing!" Steckle's eyes were on the EKG
monitor, which still exhibited a flatline. "Not a
goddamn—"

"Up me to three hundred," ordered Labraccio. He grabbed the defib paddles with their
increased current, and rubbed them together.
"Clear!"

Another jolt of current sent Nelson Wright's
dead body surging off the gurney. The EKG
monitor showed—flatline.

"CPR!" Labraccio thrust the paddles back into
the girl's hands, and she recharged them with
fresh current. David began to press the heels of
his hands rhythmically into Nelson's breast-
bone, doing cardiopulmonary resuscitation.

"One-one-thousand, two-one-thousand, three-one-thousand—"

"Ninety-eight degrees," Rachel Mannus reported.

"Hit him again," Labraccio ordered. "Three-fifty."

"Nothing," moaned Steckle miserably. "Oh, shit!"

Hurley brought the video camera in close, leaning forward for the closeup on Nelson's empty face. Again, the charged defibs zapped hard against Nelson's chest. Again, the body bucked up, fell back.

Nelson wasn't "It" anymore. Somebody else was, and they had to find him. The boys were yelling now, and the dog Champ was barking like crazy and getting under everybody's feet. It was kind of a hide-and-seek game now, only different, and Nelson was leading the way, the other boys following as he ran towards the trees.

The trees were tall, taller than Nelson remembered . . . remembered? Had he been here before? Were these trees a new experience or a memory? Massive they were, with rough bark and strong limbs, but no branch stood nearer to the ground than twenty feet. At the top, the tree limbs wore a massed crown of dark leaves, like a giant with black hair. The nine-year-old Nelson didn't like those trees. He didn't want to go near them, but—

That face! High up in the branches, that face! A child's face, yet not a child's, something infinitely more grotesque than a child's. Nelson's skin crawled with disbelief. It couldn't be, couldn't!

Blip. The flatline jumped suddenly, and a tiny peak formed. The EKG monitor suddenly showed a little electronic heart, like a scoreboard at a baseball game, only this was no game. Joe Hurley turned his camera on it instantly, then swung the lens back to Nelson. "Got him!" he yelled, triumphant.

"O-2!" barked Labraccio, and Randall Steckle slapped the oxygen mask over Nelson's face.

"Eppy, in!" But Rachel Mannus was ahead of him; anticipating the need, she was already injecting one cc of the stimulant epinephrine into the IV in Nelson's arm. "In," she said.

They watched now, unable to tear themselves away from the body on the gurney, waiting to see the miracle they might just have worked. One by one, vital signs appeared. Color coming into the white face. The eyelids fluttering. The smallest movement of the head.

"He's in REM sleep now. We got him," whispered David.

Suddenly, Nelson Wright's eyes blinked open. He looked around, seeing his classmates staring at him with unbelieving eyes, noting with amusement that Steckle was drenched in sweat, that Hurley had lost his vaunted cool, that Labraccio was trembling slightly, and that Rachel's eyes were even larger than ever, while her dark, thick hair was plastered to her forehead with perspiration. He smiled.

"Nelson, Nelson, can you hear us?" cried Rachel.

"Nelson, you crazy motherfucker!" whooped Joe, delirious with excitement. "You did it!"

Nelson Wright nodded weakly, unable to speak. His mouth was as dry as cotton thanks to the drugs, and his head hurt. The intravenous adrenaline had the heart jumping in his chest. But he could see the astonishment and relief in the others' faces, and it made him proud. It had worked. His mad doctor experiment hadn't been so crazy after all. Nelson Wright had died and come back from the dead. He'd had his look-see. Something was definitely out there. And, look, he was back, and none the worse for it.

They carried him out of the Dog Lab like a hero, wrapped in a blanket to keep his body temperature stable at ninety-eight point six. All of them were weak with relief and a great sense of triumph. See what they'd done! They'd brought someone back from the dead! What power they had!

Nelson Wright, exhausted, exalted, unable to stop smiling, stumbled along between Joseph Hurley and Randall Steckle, while David Labraccio and Rachel Mannus followed behind. They carried him past the painted murals of Hippocrates and Galen, of Vesalius and Harvey, of Lister and the others.

He was one of them now, in the pantheon of the immortals of medicine, a man who had broken through to the other side, who had returned bearing sacred wisdom for mankind. Nelson Wright, hero, the colleague and equal of Hippocrates. For the first time, a human being had sought to make the journey into death under controlled conditions, witnessed and detailed with scientific accuracy.

He was Lazarus, raised from the dead by Jesus. He was Orpheus, who descended to the underworld to bring back Eurydice. He was Prometheus, who had dared to steal the fire of the gods and bring it back to humankind.

Of course Prometheus had been punished for his dastardly hubris. The outraged gods had him chained spread-eagled to a rock for all eternity, while vultures pecked out his liver. What the gods own they want to keep for themselves. It is in the immortals' creed that there are some things humankind is better off not chasing after.

The cold night air made Nelson shiver, and he pulled the blanket more tightly around him. His body hadn't yet adjusted to the temperature difference. Only a few minutes ago, he'd been racing across a meadow in the heat of an August sun. Now he was back in late October under a harvest moon.

In the sky, the ever-changing moon, ghostly companion of the virgin huntress Artemis, shone down full, lighting the strange triumphal procession. In its millions of years of circling the Earth, Earth's satellite had seen many peculiar things, but none more peculiar than this.

"You walked on the moon!" Joe praised,

caught up in the glow of the moment.

"Do you know how big this is?" Steckle murmured in wonder. "Can you even imagine? You trespassed on the gods!" Steckle's words were actually more prophetic than he knew, for the gods take the trespass of mortals not lightly, and their anger is terrible.

Witness Prometheus.

Labraccio's canvas-covered truck was parked a block down from Taft; the little group headed for it and, when they reached it, they let Nelson down on the tailgate. His knees trembled a little, but only briefly. The cool October night was clearing his head of the drugs that had been pumped into his system, and he was starting to feel a little stronger, but he was still treading the infinite.

"Thanks for saving me," he told the group.

"Can you remember any of it?" It was the one question uppermost in all their minds, but Rachel was the first to voice it.

"Can you recall any specific emotion or sensation? Heat? Cold? Anything like that?" Hurley's face was alight with curiosity.

Nelson smiled. He was still wrapped in exaltation, but he knew that this was his moment. He'd been completely vindicated, and he intended to make the most of it.

"No, it's an experience that can't be broken down into specifics."

"Did you see a tunnel with a light at the end of it?" Rachel wanted to know.

Nelson looked around at the curious young

faces of his companions; they were enthralled, hanging on his every word. His smile grew broader, then he set his own young face into serious lines, and lowered his voice for maximum effect.

"There is something out there," he said slowly, and the others felt a chill at his words, and they shivered.

The wind rose suddenly, sending clouds racing before it to obscure the moon. The night grew darker. The scent of impending rain was in the air. An uneasiness swept over the group; the night seemed all at once a lot colder. They stopped talking and began to pile into David's truck. Suddenly they were starving.

By the time they reached the nearest convenience store, Nelson Wright had lapsed into silence. He sat huddled in the blanket inside the tailgate of the moving truck, staring up at the moon as it appeared and disappeared behind the scudding clouds. His face was rapt, concentrating.

When Joe, Randy and Rachel disappeared into the store to buy munchies and soda, David wrapped the blood pressure cuff around Nelson's arm and took a reading. Ninety over seventy-five. Low, but that was expected. It would increase. His friend's silence was disturbing, since Nelson always had some cynical wisecrack or a piece of his own unique dark philosophy to impart.

"Are you okay, O Wise One?" he joked, but Nelson didn't smile. His face in the moonlight seemed very young, his eyes far away and un-readable.

"Labraish, I feel like a highly tuned radio," he breathed. "Listen, can you hear the traffic on 128?"

David bent over the blood pressure gauge to see it more clearly. "Uh-huh."

"Now, beneath that, there's a hum. It's from the street lamps."

The street lamps? David Labraccio looked up, mildly surprised. But Nelson's expression was perfectly serious, and he had his head to one side, listening with absorption. Letting the air out, hissing, from the gauge, David listened, too. For an instant he heard nothing, then he became aware of a faint buzzing from the tall mercury vapor street lamps. It was usually undetectable, because usually nobody was interested in detecting it. But Nelson was right; the sound was there.

"All right," he smiled.

Nelson's voice dropped. "Now even fainter . . ." he said in a near whisper. "There's some kind of dragging sound."

Labraccio listened intently for it, but heard nothing. It seemed obvious to him that Nelson's heightened perceptions were a result of the heavy cocktail of drugs they'd shot into him, and the convulsive electrical punishment his body had taken, added to his brain's temporary oxygen deprivation. What Nelson Wright had just gone through was enough to change the perceptions of an elephant.

"Sorry."

"It's getting louder," insisted Nelson. "I can not only hear it, I can feel it. Like a little boy, dragging a stick behind him as he delivers his morning papers."

David looked sharply at his friend, but Nelson Wright's face was perfectly serious. He shook his head, and stuffed the blood pressure monitor into Nelson's coat pocket. "Well, your prognosis is excellent, and I'm hungry. You'll look great on *60 Minutes*, 'Doctor Death.'"

Nelson Wright shook his head. "It's bigger than that," he said in a low tone.

Labraccio grinned. "When you're through with it, I'm sure it will be. Can I get you something?"

"No, no, go ahead." Nelson Wright looked shrewdly at his friend. "You're not buying any of this, are you?"

Labraccio hesitated, giving the question his full attention. Nelson was right. It was true. Whatever it was that Nelson might believe he had encountered Out There, David's rational mind would attribute to the nitrous, or the epinephrine, or the adrenalin, or the potent combination of all three.

As for scientific curiosity, David Labraccio had as large a quota as anybody, but he believed firmly that death was it, the Big D, *finito*, the end. Death was rightfully inevitable, a natural event that physicians fought to postpone, but never conquered. It would take a lot more than a medical student's drug trip to convince him otherwise.

"Hey, you forget I'm an atheist," he said lightly. "You be all right for a few minutes?"

Nelson nodded, and wrapped the blanket around him a little tighter, burrowing down into its folds. David smiled, and vanished into the convenience store, intent on a bag of Doritos.

"How's he doin'?" asked Joe Hurley.

"He's physically stable, but he talks like Lazarus come back from the dead," said Labraccio with a shrug.

"Well that's what we did, right?" Hurley's blue eyes crackled with excitement, and he sounded high. "We brought him back from the dead."

"We got lucky," Labraccio said.

"Seriously, why shouldn't we all get famous for this?" pressed Joe.

"You'll all be famous," snapped David. "They'll build monuments to you. Little stone ones, about so high. 'Rest in Peace.'"

"I want to go next."

They all turned to stare at Rachel, startled by her sudden declaration.

"I want to do it," she said staunchly, not flinching from her classmates' surprise.

"Hey, why should you and Nelson hog all the glory?" cried Joe. "We're the guys that brought the dog back." He jerked his thumb at Randall Steckle. "We'll go next."

"We"! Again with the "'we"! Where the hell was he getting this "we"? "Ah . . . Joe . . . I think . . ."

stammered Steckle, really worried, but Hurley interrupted him.

"Like it or not, I'm going next," insisted Joe.

Rachel Mannus drew in a deep breath. "I would be willing to go under for one minute and twenty seconds," she said boldly.

"One thirty," retorted Hurley instantly.

Rachel glared at him angrily. Joe glared back. "All right, one forty," he added.

Rachel stood silent, temporarily defeated. It was settled, then. Joe Hurley would be next, and he'd stay dead for a minute and forty seconds before the others would begin to revive him.

Randall Steckle was furious. The madness seemed to him to be escalating. They were all talking like fools. Sure, they'd been lucky with Nelson, but it could easily have gone the other way. Nelson could have died on the table, and they'd all have been fucked. The time to quit was now, while they were ahead.

"Are you all crazy, or just so goddamn competitive that you would enter into a bidding war with your lives?" he growled.

Rachel Mannus kept her silence, her face like stone.

Hurley cocked his head insolently. "Well, that's it, then. One forty. Not a bad price to pay for stock in fame and glory."

"Die to be a hero if you have to, but don't die to be a celebrity," said Labraccio in disgust.

While the others argued inside the convenience store, Nelson Wright sat alone in the moonlight, his feet dangling over the tailgate, his coat wrapped tightly around him and the blanket pulled over his shoulders. He felt completely alive; every sense was alert and functioning at the highest efficiency, yet, paradoxically, he also felt more at peace than he'd ever felt in his life. His mind kept returning to his death experience, and a large part of him wanted to be back there . . . needed to be back there.

All the while he was thinking, he was conscious of the dragging sound. It seemed to be growing louder and louder, coming closer and closer. Louder and louder. Closer and closer. And it was now accompanied by a terrible low whining, as from some dumb animal in agony.

Suddenly, around the corner and into the light of the street lamp, a dog dragged itself. A medium-sized dog of no particular breed, a spotted mongrel with floppy ears. Apparently injured in its hindquarters, it was bandaged and matted with blood and its back legs trailed uselessly behind it. When it saw Nelson, the dog subsided on its rump in the gutter and stared at him. Under the yellow street light, its eyes looked like two empty holes in its grotesque head.

Nelson couldn't take his eyes off the animal; he felt a great surge of pity . . . and of something else . . . something he couldn't identify . . . a nagging something.

"Puppy?" he called softly. "Puppy? What happened? Doggie?"

The dog never moved, but its empty eyes never left Nelson's face. It kept its gaze locked on his, as though neither one of them could bear to tear it away.

"Puppy? Pup?"

The wind rose again, making Nelson shiver with cold.

"Champ?" he whispered.

Perhaps moved by the icy wind, or maybe summoned by the whispered name, the dog began to move slowly forward. It couldn't walk, but it half-crawled, half-slithered toward Nelson. The effort was painfully terrible; a thick foam of saliva formed on the dog's jaws and slobbered onto its matted breast. Its hindquarters began to bleed with fresh blood. As it came it kept up that painful whining.

Nelson's brain now identified the nagging feeling. It was fear. An irrational fear of a helpless, wounded animal . . . an animal covered in blood, and without eyes. He was dreadfully afraid.

"Stay," he croaked in a hoarse whisper. "Stay, Champ. Champ, stop."

But the dog kept coming, slowly, dragging itself painfully across the gutter an inch at a time, yet covering the distance between them. Nelson began backing away, further and further into the depths of the truck. He never thought of the others, within earshot in the store. From the moment he saw the dog, Nelson and the animal had eyes for nobody but each other. Their eyes seemed bonded together.

Suddenly, a car came around the corner. It

was heading straight for the dog; the driver couldn't possibly see it, crouched down on its belly in the dark street. The mongrel was going to be run over.

"No!" yelled Nelson, as the speeding automobile bore down.

Behind him he heard voices and laughter. Nelson turned. The other medical students were coming out of the store with paper bags. The wheels of the car sped by, and Nelson turned again, bracing for the awful crunch and the yelp of anguish.

But there was nothing. No dog, no agonized yelping, no sickening thud or the sound of wheels rolling over flesh and bone. There was only the car, disappearing harmlessly around the next corner. The street was empty.

"Somebody ought to stay with him," said Labraccio. "He's still pretty shaky."

"I have class in a few hours," Steckle said quickly, and Hurley said nothing.

"I will," Rachel volunteered.

Hurley grinned knowingly at Steckle, who raised one of his bushy eyebrows significantly. Catching this exchange, Rachel chose not to dignify it with a comment.

"All right, Rachel stays," said Labraccio. He looked anxiously at Nelson, who appeared to have lost some ground while they were in the store. His face was drawn, his eyes staring, and, despite the cold, little beads of sweat had formed on his forehead.

"You okay?"

Nelson let out his breath. "Yeah. Yeah, I'm okay," he said in a flat voice. "I'd like to go home now."

He leaned back against the canvas wall of the truck and allowed himself to relax a little, forcing his fists to unclench, but all the way home, Nelson Wright shook with a nameless fear.

Rachel didn't feel sleepy at all; she was wide awake, incredibly excited, watching in fascination and taking notes in her little secret notebook as Nelson tossed and turned in his bed. He was obviously dreaming, and made small moaning noises in his sleep.

In his dream Nelson had gone Back There, back to the hot sunlight of his ninth summer. He was running, running across an empty meadow, and he could hear the other two running and laughing with him. Champ kept getting in the way, running under his feet, his ears flopping as he scampered, barking happily in his vigorous puppyhood, just glad to be alive and running with Nelson. It was a wonderful hide-and-seek game they were playing, the boys and the dog.

"Ollie ollie oxen-free!" yelled Scotty, signaling the end of hide-and-seek. "Get him, Champ. Find him, boy."

"Come out, come out, wherever you are!" Hank added his voice to Scotty's. But Billy was still hiding. Billy wouldn't come out, not even to ollie ollie oxen-free, the universally-acknowledged home free. Billy Mahoney didn't believe in home free.

Nelson whimpered in his sleep and rolled over on his back, throwing one arm over his brow as though to block out memory. Rachel leaned forward in her chair, observing him anxiously by the dim light of the small bedside lamp.

"Are you okay?" she asked softly as Nelson opened his eyes.

"Why?" Half sitting up, Nelson shook his groggy head to clear it.

"You were hyperventilating." Her long slim fingers touched the base of Nelson's throat, checking his pulse, and her sweet grave face concentrated on the sweep second hand of her watch. Satisfied, she entered the reading in her notebook. "We can expect your blood pressure to rise slowly over the next fourteen hours, as the cardio valves—"

Rachel broke off as Nelson's hand reached out and touched the soft waves of her long dark hair.

"You're very beautiful," he breathed.

She pulled away from his touch. "We'll talk later," the girl said uncomfortably, embarrassed as she always was when a boy came on to her. Rachel wanted desperately to be taken seriously, not regarded as a potential lay. If she hated anything about herself, it was her beauty, which always seemed to get between her and the other person. Pocketing her notebook, she stood up to leave the room. "Get some rest."

Nelson Wright sat all the way up in bed, his head resting against the lacquered white wall. On his face was that special smile of his, too brilliant, and his green eyes glittered. "I'll bet that twenty-four hours ago you never thought you'd be spending the night here," he teased.

Rachel stiffened. "You were lucky last night," she said curtly. "Don't push it."

Nelson watched her leave the room, striding with unconscious grace. He grinned. Lucky indeed, he thought. Lucky, lucky Nelson Wright.

CHAPTER 5

He wasn't going to chicken out. Joe Hurley had given his word to the others and he couldn't back out now without suffering total humiliation. One minute forty seconds he'd promised, and one forty he'd live up to. Live up to, that was a laugh. Die up to, more likely.

After all, no living thing is immortal; even rocks eventually die. But why rush the process? Joe Hurley had everything to lose—his youth, his charming good looks, all those ripe and willing young girls, his love for Anne, his impending marriage, his graduation with honors, a long and profitable career in medicine, the Porsche—everything a man could want. Was any of it worth giving up just for a chance at . . . what? Fame? Being the second one to go? And maybe the first one not to come back? Joe could surely be allowed a few frightened and sobering second thoughts in the cold light of the morning after.

Joe had gone to bed the night before in a state of high elation, but he woke up in a state of low funk. He was scared shitless. Already he regretted his impulsive decision, but there was no way that he could back out of it without being shown up for a coward. So he'd go. He wasn't ready to die. He hadn't made preparations. If anything went wrong, would his death count against him as a mortal sin, as suicide?

He wasn't the world's best Catholic, and he hadn't been to confession in a very long time, because he didn't want to tell a priest about the tapes, and have to stop doing them. But he did believe in God, and his family was religious. What would they tell his family? That their son had actually chosen to die? How would they explain it to his fiancée?

Anne. It didn't matter what he did with other girls; Anne was the only one he loved, she was the girl he was pledged to marry. Anne. He needed to see her, talk to her. Hurley wasn't given overmuch to introspection; life and its creature comforts had always been taken for granted. He'd been born smart, good-looking and lucky, and had been blessed by the leprechauns with legendary Irish charm. Joe had never had to think about life very much; only two things ruled him—his competitiveness and his crotch. He hadn't begun to realize the extent of the calming and stabilizing influence a girl like Anne Colgen had on him, but this morning he felt its absence strongly.

Wearing only his Jockey underwear, Joe padded across his bedroom floor to his television set on the far side of the loft bedroom. He opened the cabinet above it. As usual when he looked into it, he couldn't hold back a complacent smile.

Arranged neatly in alphabetical order in Joe Hurley's cabinet were the precious secret videotapes he'd made with his own camcorder, labeled from "Andrea" to "Yael." Here was a filmed record of his sexual encounters, Joe hard at play in bed with some of the prettiest girls in town, captured on tape for his later enjoyment. Here were Veronica, Jane, Brenda, Mona, Donna, Pauline and all the others, their breasts and thighs, their moans and whimpers of passion, all captured and preserved through the miracle of Japanese technology.

None of the girls had been aware she was being videotaped having sex with Joe. He never told them. Every one of them had been lured into bed by Joe's charm, Joe's good looks, Joe's hot body, Joe's quick wit and clever one-liners, his compliments and flattery. They'd come willingly to get laid, but would they have come so willingly if they'd known they were going to star in a fuck movie? Joe knew the answer to that one. But he didn't feel guilty. He'd shown each and every one of them a good time, a satisfying

time. And if he never called any of them again
. . . so what? He hadn't done them any harm,
had he? No.

In the drawer next to his sex tapes were other
tapes, tapes he could take out and show at family
gatherings, tapes he could even let his mother
see. He thought of them as "G" rated.

His fingers trailed along the videotape boxes
until he found the one he was looking for, the
tape labeled "Engagement Party, July 1989."
Pulling it out, Joe fed it to the VCR, and curled
up in his brokendown easy chair to watch it.

Whenever he watched this videotape and saw
his friends and relatives laughing, dancing,
drinking Irish toasts to the engaged pair, having
a swell time, tears would fill his eyes. Joe always
snuffled a little when he saw the beautiful couple that he and his blond Anne made—good-
looking, devoted, wholesome, suited to each
other. Joe's easy tears had nothing to do with
emotion, only with sentiment. So far in his life
he'd rarely felt a true emotion, shying away from
them as though they had sharks' teeth, living
only for the moment and determined to make
every moment count.

Watching the home video now and feeling
sorry for himself, dreading tonight's experiment
for which he'd volunteered, Joe wallowed in his
sentimental thoughts of Anne, and a sudden
longing to hear her voice washed over him. If
only he could tell her! She'd know how to
comfort him and make him less afraid.

Punching out the telephone number of Anne's sorority house, Joe felt a little better. While he waited for her to come to the hall phone, he composed himself. He couldn't possibly tell her. He knew with certainty that he could not let Anne know about Nelson's experiment, and definitely not that he himself had volunteered to go next. Instead, they made boy-girl–twosome chatter for a few minutes.

"I'm counting the days to Thanksgiving," he told her.

"I know," bubbled Anne. "I can't wait." In the background, Joe could hear the voices of other girls; there was little if any privacy on the sorority phone. "I've got to transfer to a school closer to you, or get a faster car."

Joe hesitated. "Sometimes I wonder . . ." he said slowly. "Maybe we should have gotten married last summer."

"My mother wasn't ready yet," laughed Anne.

Joe knew that Anne's mother—and Anne, too—looked forward to a big church wedding with the Monsignor presiding and a white wedding album and all the trimmings, and that took time to plan and set up. They didn't want some quickie ceremony with only two bridesmaids and no canvas tent.

"You know you're the best." His voice was barely audible, and the girl had to press the receiver tightly to her ear to hear it. "If anything should ever happen . . ."

"Joey! What's wrong?" Alarm made Anne's

voice shrill. What did he mean by "anything" and "ever happen"?

Joe realized at once that he'd gone just a little too far. He wanted her sympathy and comfort, but he hadn't meant to trigger anxieties in Anne. He backed off, confused. "I don't know . . . I'm just so tired. I should go, I'm not really making sense. . . ."

"Joe? Joe? You're scaring me! What's wrong?"

"Nothing's wrong. I love you." Joe Hurley hung up the telephone, feeling worse than ever.

The full harvest moon was playing catch-me with low clouds, which held the promise of rain. The sky was an inky black. The wind off Lake Michigan cut like a scalpel, flaying skin and flesh and reaching through to the bone. In weather like this, the campus was always deserted. You had to be a fool to cross vast empty spaces at night, where the icy winds could find you.

At eleven that night the five of them, shivering with cold, gathered in the Dog Lab for what Steckle told his tape recorder dramatically was "Day 99, medical roulette, chamber two, Hurley's turn with the gun." Hurley, who would normally have found Steckle's adlibs hysterical, wasn't laughing.

Having already witnessed Nelson Wright's journey into death the evening before, the group was somewhat more subdued and more focused now, and more matter-of-fact. Joe stripped quickly and climbed up onto the gurney without his usual ribald wisecracking and even without calling Rachel's attention to his muscular young body.

But he didn't want to go out looking chicken. Picking up the EEG electrodes, Hurley gave them a feeble wave, and tried a small joke. "And now to board the interstellar cruiser."

Rachel stepped up quietly and attached the suction cups to his head, then connected the EKG to Joe's arms, legs and heart, all with her customary cool efficiency. Joe reached for Randy Steckle and pulled his old buddy's ear close to his own lips.

"If anything happens to me, burn the tapes," he whispered urgently.

"You can count on me, Mr. Nixon." But Steckle looked genuinely worried, his face crumpling a little, like a child's. His fingers fiddled nervously with the strap on his mini audio recorder. As the official chronicler of Joseph Patrick Hurley's experimental journey into death he was also loaded down with Joe's camcorder.

Perhaps there was somewhat less drama in the sight of Joe Hurley going under because the others had seen it before. But the fear was still there with them, and maybe even stronger. With Nelson, they'd never been sure that they were really going through with letting him stay dead for an entire minute. But with Joe, they knew they were all committed to a minute and forty seconds, a heavy number. Also, with Nelson, maybe they'd just been lucky. Who knew if their luck would hold tonight?

For what seemed the longest time, Joe's body processes slowed down but did not stop. The monitors kept showing a wave pattern record of his vital signs, and the transcribing needles kept printing them out. At last, the EKG uttered its shrill mechanical scream, signaling that no more blips would be issuing from it.

"Flatline," Rachel Mannus said quietly. The first stage. Death of the heart.

"Yes," Steckle said into his little tape recorder. "That's confirmed asystole, which is what we're doing here. There is tension . . . there is fear . . . as Mr. 'L' removes the oxygen mask. . . ."

David Labraccio took the mask off Joe's face, while Nelson leaned over to switch off the annoying tone of the EKG. The six lines on the EEG monitor hooked up to Joe's head continued to scribble away, measuring his diminishing brain waves. The lines grew flatter and flatter, moving toward flatline, and the monitor kept uttering shorter and less frequent blips. Randy Steckle moved in nearer for a tight closeup of Joe's silent face.

"This is okay," he said, still recording. "Everything is fine. Subject 'J' lies peacefully. Quite a study. A fascinating study . . ."

"You're babbling, Steckle," snapped Nelson.

"He does that," David said.

The blips on the EEG monitor ceased; the line flattened and ran straight across the screen, uttering a whine. Deprived of vital oxygen, Joe's brain quietly suffocated.

"He's dead," said Rachel as she checked the second hand on her wristwatch. One forty had begun.

"Oh, boy," moaned Steckle, sweating profusely. "That's cessation of all brain function. Absence of all . . . uh . . . reflexes."

His first thought was that there should be a lot more light. Others who'd gone before and come back had reported a beautiful and welcoming white light. He could see light somewhere at a distance, but it seemed to be very far off, and wasn't overwhelming; it didn't cover him over in radiance. His second awareness was of flesh— warm, soft, female flesh. Bare flesh was everywhere around Joe, enfolding him in its perfumed fragrance. And milk, milk from a gigantic sweet nipple. Mother's milk, delicious!

Others who had returned from the brink had reported that the tunnel to the light was lined with gone-before loved ones, smiling a welcome and urging them upward with arms wide open. But Joe's open-armed loved ones were all women, beautiful women, voluptuous women with big breasts, long legs and tight behinds in short skirts. All of them were smiling at Joe, blowing kisses, showing Joe their tantalizing tongues, making him aware by their wanton gestures that they desired him. None of them seemed to be dead or gone-before; every one of them was vibrant with life, pulsating with life. It made him hard just to look at them.

If this is a dream, don't let me wake up, he prayed.

He could see himself now with all of them, making love to them, going from one to the next in his journey toward the beckoning light. He was stripping off the flimsy lacy brassieres to bury his face in those luscious knockers, pulling down satin g-string panties to find a home between those silken thighs. Some of the women he recognized as girls he'd had; others were *Playboy* centerfolds he'd jacked off to when he was thirteen—oh, Christ, there was Miss October! And she was even more fantastic than he remembered.

He thought of an old joke, about a guy who dies and comes back to see his friend. The friend asks, "What's it like?" and the guy says, "Oh, it's not so bad. I get up in the morning and I fuck, have breakfast, then fuck, take a nap, then fuck, then lunch, then a fuck—" and the friend says, "That's heaven?" And the guy says, "What heaven? I'm a jackrabbit in Arizona!"

That's death, thought Joe happily, seizing another pair of thighs. I'm a jackrabbit in Arizona.

The closer he moved to the beckoning light, the younger Joe seemed to become. High school. He was back in high school, endlessly horny, making out in the back of his dad's car with Mary Catherina Tognazzi. He felt the fuzz of her sweater as a sense-memory under his fingers; he could experience again the angora giving way to the feel of bare young breast, and how he'd come all over himself. God, what a great feeling!

Now he was younger still, and the girls were younger, too, with long hair and tiny budding breasts beneath virginal starched white parochial school blouses. Joe felt once more the awkwardness of stealing a kiss from a girl whose tender lips covered a set of orthodontic braces. There were stirrings inside him that he was really too young to experience. The girls with him were too young to be enticing, yet they enticed. Their eyes glittered with lust, and their baby hands reached out to him. . . .

"One minute twenty," said Rachel.

"Okay," Nelson said. "Time to bring him back home."

There were almost too many women. In his wildest dreams Joe Hurley had never imagined that there could ever be too many women, but there almost were. He was rolling in naked flesh, drowning in it, it was stifling him. Beautiful women, all of them hungry. Too hungry. Hungry for Joe. He felt all-powerful; as soon as one sapped his energy, there was more energy for the next woman. It felt good, though, so very, very good . . .

He wasn't responding. Joe Hurley was lying on his back, not responding, his vital signs still two sets of deadly flatlines. Something terrible was about to happen, Steckle thought in horror.

They were going to lose his old pal Hurley.

Zap! The defib paddles slammed into Joe's chest, two hundred joules, three hundred, three-fifty. Nothing.

"Nothing!" yelled Nelson. "Starting CPR." His hands got busy, trying to prime Joe's heart to start beating. "One-one-thousand, two-one-thousand, three-one-thousand, breathe!" He worked harder. "Four-one-thousand, five-one-thousand, c'mon, Joe, breathe!"

Panic had them all by the throat. One forty, why the hell had they agreed to let him go one forty? It was longer than that now; they'd been working him over more than a minute, but Joe Hurley was still dead on the table.

"Atropine in," reported Labraccio. Three of them were working furiously on Joe, fighting to revive him while Steckle continued to film.

"What's going on here?" cried Nelson, and sweat began to run down his face. He continued cardiopulmonary resuscitation, pressing down rhythmically on Joe's chest with the heels of his hands, and starting the count again at one.

"Three-one-thousand, four-one-thousand, five-one-thousand," muttered Nelson desperately as he pounded on Hurley's chest and rocked his sternum. "Breathe, damn you, Joe, breathe!"

Steckle aimed his camera at the EKG monitor. There was no change. "Nothing, flat," he said in a hoarse whisper. "CPR and atropine, but not a thing."

Her hands trembling a little, Rachel checked the IV and the blanket. Nelson continued CPR, his shoulders moving to a steady rhythm as he pumped his hands into Joe's chest cavity.

"What's the matter here?" Nelson Wright yelled at Joe's unhearing body. "C'mon, man, c'mon!" His hands faltered for a second, then picked up the beat, harder than ever. Sweat glistened on his forehead, darkening his blond hair where it fell forward into his eyes.

Behind Nelson's back, David and Rachel exchanged worried glances. If this didn't work . . .

Sighing, Labraccio stepped forward. "Nelson, let me try it," he said in a low voice.

Wright looked up angrily; sweat was stinging his eyes, and he could barely see Labraccio. "I'm doing everything I can," he growled at David.

"We're running out of time," said Rachel urgently.

"Yeah, let Dave try!" pleaded Steckle.

"Step back, Nelson," Rachel put in quietly.

Three against one. Furious, Nelson moved back from the gurney and gave his place to David, who picked up the CPR beat calmly and without effort. All Nelson could do was glare at him jealously, at the confidence with which Dave worked, the easy familiarity with which Rachel worked alongside him, the two of them functioning as a unit, a team.

"One-one-thousand, two-one-thousand, three-one-thousand . . ." But it wasn't working. The monitors still showed flatlines.

The atmosphere in the Dog Lab was heavy with unspoken dread. It didn't seem possible that Joe Hurley could really stay dead; not Joe, with everything going for him. Cocksure, grinning, teasing Joe, who enjoyed playing the clown, who loved medicine almost as much as his reflection in a full-length mirror—that Joe Hurley couldn't be dead.

It didn't seem possible; nevertheless, he wasn't responding. Nothing they tried seemed to be working. What were they going to do?

"We're dead," whispered Steckle, staring at the monitors.

"Five-one-thousand, breathe!" urged David. "C'mon, Joe, I know you're in there. Breathe!"

Something fluttered under his hand. Was it possible? A breath? Or just a numbness in David Labraccio's palm? No, there it was again, more noticeable this time! Joe's chest had moved, had taken in air. A heart was beginning to beat!

Blip! The sweetest sound in all the world, that little electronic blip. The EKG electrodes moved; the lines on the heart monitor wavered, jumped once, twice . . . peaked, jumped again. Vital signs had returned, were now being measured, recorded, printed out on paper just as though Joe's returning from the dead was some ordinary event and not a miracle.

"O-2," snapped Labraccio.

"O-2 up," affirmed Rachel as she placed the oxygen mask over Hurley's nose and mouth. "It's okay, Joe. You're going to be okay."

"Yeah!" yelled Randy Steckle happily, nearly dropping Joe's camcorder.

Rachel's eyes met David's and they exchanged a smile of pride and satisfaction and mutual

94

respect. Seeing the smile, Nelson Wright felt a hand squeezing his heart.

"We did it!" Steckle crowed, a little inaccurately. "We got him! CPR successful. Hurley lives!"

Labraccio saw the look of resentment on Nelson's face. Sensitive to Nelson's moods, he immediately realized that his friend felt strongly that it should have been he and not David who brought Joe back. The whole experiment had been Nelson's in the first place. Now it must seem to him that the others had virtually elbowed him aside.

"Nelson . . ." he began apologetically, but Nelson only turned away and shoved an ampule of atropine into Joe's IV.

And then suddenly there was Joe Hurley opening his big blue eyes and grinning. Then he was coughing a little, and blinking and trying to sit up, and somehow any resentment became lost in the triumph of the moment.

— CHAPTER 6 —

I t was great," said Joe.
  "Here it comes." David Labraccio grinned with some cynicism. Hurley would now begin to embroider and romanticize his experience. Nothing Joe ever did was less than great; none of his encounters with women less than fantastic.
  "Why don't you just let him talk, Dave?" asked Nelson Wright, never taking his eyes off Hurley's face, as though searching for answers in Joe's blue eyes.
  "Define 'great,'" Rachel said, taking another sip of her coffee. The five medical students were sitting around a table in an otherwise empty all-night diner. Joe, pale and tired and wrapped in a blanket, was the center of attention, and

obviously having a ball with it.

"I don't know. It's difficult to explain, maybe impossible," Joe began hesitantly. " 'Great' means not thinking about the past, or the future. 'Great' means just feeling here, now." He wondered if he was making any sense.

"Yeah," Labraccio broke in cynically, "dying is funny that way."

Joe turned his face to Labraccio. He sounded serious, even a little spiritual, something of a first for Hurley. "Dave, Nelson's right. There's something out there, activity beyond death."

"Absolutely," confirmed Nelson, as the others leaned forward eagerly in their seats, hanging on every word.

"The experience," continued Joe, "was a little strange . . . almost erotic."

"He's dead and he gets laid," joked Randy Steckle.

Nelson Wright frowned. Erotic? What was Hurley talking about? His own experience could not be described in any way as erotic. It was not erotic in the slightest degree. "Erotic?" he asked out loud. "What do you mean, erotic?"

Joe backed down quickly, realizing that he had mouthed himself into an embarrassing situation, and afraid that he would shock or repel his classmates by the steamy details. "Just a little. I don't want you to think that it was casually, wantonly sexual, by any means."

"That would never have occurred to me, not in a million years. No way." Steckle

98

shook his head in a mixture of amusement and envy.

"But there was an energy which I could feel, which felt like heat on the outside and love on the inside. It was friendly," insisted Joe.

"I think you just redefined 'Big Bang,'" joked David. It was obvious that he was still skeptical where the near-death experience was concerned.

"No, really," insisted Joe. "I think that there was something friendly and vaguely feminine guiding me." "Vaguely feminine," yes, if those were the words to describe naked breasts and buttocks.

Nelson Wright sat back in his chair and his frown deepened into a scowl. His thoughts went racing. Plainly, Joe Hurley's near-death experience had almost nothing in common with his own. Even the feelings it aroused were different. Nelson had seen himself as a boy again. Joe had been guided by females. What did that mean? Could it possibly signify that there might be no universal experience common to all, no actual post-death event that might be scientifically verified, recorded as fact and pass into the textbooks? What if there were no more than a subjective series of near-death experiences, different for everybody? *An* experience rather than *the* experience? Wouldn't that make his research less scientifically valid, his experiments less earth-shattering? Wouldn't it take something away from his future glory?

But the others were still too wrapped up in Joe's narrative to notice the expression on Nelson's face.

"This is the conquest of our generation!" enthused Steckle, his eyes sparkling behind the thick lenses of his eyeglasses, his round cheeks glowing red. "The last great frontier. First you had the sea, then America, the West, the moon, Mr. Leary, drugs, the inner journey. Then Miss MacLaine, our illustrious former First Lady and the outer journey. But this is ours!" He jumped clumsily out of his chair, almost knocking it over in his excitement.

"Well, we did have disco—" laughed Labraccio.

"We finally found something worthwhile!" finished Steckle happily. "Something to upstage those fuckin' baby boomers!"

"You mean *I* found something," Nelson cut in harshly. "Let's not forget that. It was *my* idea."

"Here's your check, watch your language." The waitress was middle-aged and very tired and her feet hurt. All the other tables were empty and the chairs were already stacked on top of them. If she could only get these crazy noisy kids out of her diner she'd have it all to herself, and she could maybe sit down with a cigarette and give her barking dogs a rest before she locked up for the night.

Joe Hurley smiled at her boyishly, turning on some of the Irish charm for which he was so justly famous. "Sorry, but I came back from the dead tonight."

The waitress didn't turn a single dyed hair. "Is that so? It doesn't surprise me. We had Elvis in here last night." She laid the check on the streaked formica tabletop. "You can pay when you're ready."

Rachel Mannus leaned forward and looked Joe Hurley squarely in the face. "Joe. Did you find it difficult, getting back?" she wanted to know.

"Nothing I remember." Joe shook his head.

"But he remembers everything else," Labraccio scoffed. He waved one hand dismissively. "You guys are full of shit. You lie, Nelson, and Joe here swears by it."

Nelson smiled quietly. "I wouldn't believe us either. Not until I saw it for myself." His eyes began to glitter, and his voice was very soft, insidiously soft. "How about it, Labraish?" he challenged.

"Yeah," Joe chimed in. "If you're an atheist, you have nothing to lose."

"I'm going next!" protested Rachel.

David's grin faded, and an angry scowl crossed his features. "Wait a minute! Nobody's going next. You're looking for answers here? There are no answers. I think both of you just saw what you wanted to, and nothing's been answered," he said slowly. Without knowing it, Labraccio was expressing out loud Nelson Wright's unspoken fears. "Give it up," he urged. "It's getting too dangerous."

Too dangerous. A brief silence fell, as David's words gave the others momentary pause, then

Rachel said resolutely, "We can't turn back now. It's too late. I'm going further. One fifty."

One fifty! Was she serious? After the struggle they had getting Joe back with one forty? Steckle and Hurley exchanged nervous glances, while Nelson Wright only continued to smile coldly.

"Two minutes." David Labraccio's words took them all by surprise, and they turned to stare at him in disbelief.

"Whoa! Whoa! I thought you said—" began Steckle.

"I changed my mind," answered Labraccio firmly. His mouth was set in a thin line and his eyes were unreadable. "I'll go two minutes."

"Two ten," Rachel said angrily.

"Two twenty," countered Labraccio calmly in this bizarre auction of death.

Outbid and furious, Rachel could only glare at David. Her smoky dark eyes smoldered with fury, but she said nothing.

"Well," Nelson murmured, "looks like we found a winner."

Pushing her chair back, Rachel Mannus threw some money from her pocket onto the table without looking to see how much it was, and stalked out of the diner. After a few seconds, Labraccio got up and followed her.

Nelson Wright lit a cigarette and drew in a lungful of the harsh smoke. In his mind he searched carefully for the right words, then he said rather hesitantly, "Joe, was there anything negative about your experience? Anything at all?"

The question startled Hurley, and somewhere in the back of his memory a small nagging doubt appeared. Negative. There had been something, a feeling, no more than that. But it was nothing he could verbalize, nothing he could even put his finger on. Just a kind of feeling . . .

In Greek tragedy, there is always a moment, one little heartbeat of time, in which the action freezes, and the world holds its breath. We are waiting for the hero, the tragic king, to do one thing wrong, the thing that makes the conclusion inevitable and terrible. Up to that moment, events are somehow reversible. After that single action, nothing can ever go back to where it was. Agamemnon stepping on the purple carpet, the purple reserved only for the gods. Oedipus calling down the curse on the murderer of his father, not knowing that the curse is upon his own head. Moments like these that change the course of human history.

Here was that moment. Nelson Wright reaching out with hesitation, almost ready to share. Had Joe Hurley spoken of that tiny nagging doubt, the experiments might not have continued. But we shall never know. Because Joe Hurley lied. And the inevitable was set into motion.

"No, nothing," Joe told Nelson.

"Good, good."

It had rained while they were in the diner. The rain had been threatening, on and off, for days, and now it finally fell, leaving the gutters slick and wet and gleaming, and the streetlights haloed by the dampness. It took David Labraccio a minute to catch up with Rachel Mannus on the dark and empty street. She was walking quickly, almost marching, her hands jammed tightly into her coat pockets, partly to keep them warm, and partly to keep them from trembling with anger.

"Hey, hey, hold on," Labraccio said, catching up, and he laid one hand on Rachel's arm to stop her.

Rachel didn't look around, but she pulled her arm savagely out of David's grip. "What was that in there, your idea of chivalry?" she stormed, increasing her pace. She was absolutely furious with him.

"No, absolutely not—"

"Or were you just trying to show me up?"

David pulled her around to face him. "What makes you think everything is always about you?" he asked her quietly.

"Because nobody seems to want me to go under. I don't need your protection, Labraccio."

"There seems to be a lot of speculation about what you *do* need, Mannus."

The apparent sexuality of the remark made her instantly angry. Rachel stopped and turned, glaring at David Labraccio. "Oh, yeah?" she challenged him. "And just what did *you* decide in your infinite wisdom?"

The light from the street lamp outlined her dark red hair like a halo; indignation made her eyes very wide. David looked at her as if for the first time, but it was far from the first time he'd looked at her. He knew intimately the curve of Rachel Mannus's cheek, the jut of her chin, the length of her slender neck.

"That anybody as smart and as driven as you are—and as incredibly beautiful—makes the rest of us nervous."

Rachel's brows went up and her long lashes flickered in surprise. She hadn't expected an answer like this, not one so thoughtful, complimentary and non-threatening. But she was too shy to know how to respond. She turned her face away from his questing gaze; David Labraccio's deepset steady eyes disturbed her and made her uncomfortable.

"Well, then, why did you change your mind?" she asked at last. They were walking side by side now, the anger and tension between them rapidly dissolving.

Labraccio shrugged. "I'm the skeptic, the control in the experiment," he explained. "I should go next. If there's nothing out there, I won't tell myself there is, and we'll all know there's no reason to go on any further."

"You don't believe anything that Nelson and Hurley have experienced?" she asked.

Labraccio hesitated, then shook his head. "I'm sure they've seen something, probably images from their lives discharged by a dying brain, much like a computer dumping its program," he said slowly.

But Rachel didn't accept Labraccio's reality. David Labraccio didn't have an exclusive lock on reason. "Then how do you explain the similarity

of death experiences from all over the world?"
she demanded. "Or the fact that people from
different cultures and religions see the same
things in the same order?"

David shrugged again. "I don't know," he
confessed frankly. "Maybe there's some chemical or hormone released in the brain at the time
of death that makes it more palatable to us."

"Now you're reaching," smiled Rachel.
"What if you go and there is something there?"

"Then you can kill yourself for as long as you
want," Labraccio smiled back.

Rachel's expression grew distant. "I don't
want to kill myself," she said softly, half to
herself.

"I'm glad to hear that," smiled David. "I don't
even know you . . . but I get the feeling I might
miss you." He glanced at Rachel shyly, out of the
corners of his eyes, astonished as always and
moved by how beautiful she was and how little
that beauty seemed to mean to her.

Rachel turned her face away again, in her
familiar gesture of shyness, but Labraccio could
see a small answering smile just touching the
corners of her generous mouth. "Why all this
obsession with death?" he asked her.

"It's not an obsession," denied the girl, with a
shake of her head. "It's an interest—" She
hesitated, then finished. "A personal interest."

David waited to hear more, because something inside him told him she wanted to tell him
more, but nothing more was forthcoming. If
Rachel Mannus was a young woman with se-

crets, she was one who kept her secrets well.

For a few seconds, something hung in the air between them, something almost palpable, but it began to grow dimmer, then it evaporated, leaving only a shadowy feeling behind. The moment, whatever it was, was over.

"Good night," Rachel said softly.

"'Night," nodded David.

She turned and walked away, and he stood looking after her, wondering about her, who she was really, what she wanted from life, what she was willing to do to get it, what she was unwilling to do, whether she was afraid of life, and what would make her afraid.

"Hey, can I drive you home or somewhere?" he called after her, reluctant to see her go.

"No thanks," she called over her shoulder, turned the corner and was gone.

Neither one of them noticed Nelson Wright, standing in the shadows of a nearby building, watching them. From a distance he'd not been able to hear their words, but he'd seen the looks they'd exchanged, and a dark feeling had fallen across his heart. Slowly, he started home.

CHAPTER 7

The wind had died down, leaving the night very still and cold, the moon high and large in the sky, surrounded by a corona of rainclouds. There were no stars, and the sound of traffic was distant and muted. Nelson's boot-heels clicked loudly on the deserted sidewalk, but, even though he hadn't lied to David Labraccio when he'd told him how all his senses had been sharpened, he was now too wrapped up in his own thoughts to hear his footsteps. He had much to occupy him.

He was anxious about Joe Hurley's near-death experience. Why was it so different from his own? What would Labraccio's be like? Would that one be different, too? He felt somehow let down, disappointed, and lonely, and the coppery taste of ashes filled his mouth.

Disappointment and loneliness, the feeling of being an outsider—these were not new emotions to Nelson Wright, but jealousy of a friend was. He liked Labraccio, but he was suddenly jealous of him, for more than one reason. Jealous of his calm proficiency and his confidence in the face of crisis. For the respect in which the others held him, especially Rachel. And he was jealous of the fact that he himself had chosen to die for only one minute, while Labraccio was willing to go for longer than twice that time. Was David Labraccio twice as daring as Nelson Wright? The thought gnawed at him.

When the experiments began, Nelson naturally expected that his would be the lead role, in fact the only role. He'd never anticipated that the others—Nelson was already beginning to think of the little group as the Flatliners—would want to follow him into death and beyond; rather, he'd pictured them as workshop elves, loyally dispensing IVs of sodium pentothal and standing by with the oxygen mask and the video recorder while he himself went out on the great adventure and brought back that greatest of trophies, *scientia*, Latin for knowledge.

That they'd actually go beyond him—to one forty and two twenty—and thereby rub the edges off his glory was an unbearable thought. The others would surpass him, and his genius would be forgotten in the rush. Labraccio would cop all the fame; he'd be the celebrated and admired hero, not Nelson. Nelson Wright needed that admiration and adulation, he'd counted on it to relieve the unhappy loneliness of his life. Desire for it drove him, impelling him onward through his imperfect days, making the nights possible to get through.

And there were other unbearable thoughts. Joe's near-death experience was significantly different from his own, and that might lose Nelson Wright brownie points in the fame game. Rachel Mannus was beginning to be interested in Labraccio; he could tell by their body language as they'd stood talking under the streetlight. For a year or more, Nelson himself had been achingly aware of Rachel and her serious, wide-eyed beauty; part of the satisfaction of this experiment had been getting her to take part in it, being near her. She was so beautiful, so intelligent. He saw her as his only equal, his only suitable life partner. He wanted her desperately, and now it seemed that somebody else was going to have her. His friend, David Labraccio. He couldn't stand to see that happen.

And there was something else. Something Nelson couldn't define. A sort of foreboding . . .

Now, for the first time, Nelson noticed that his steps were not leading him homeward, but in the opposite direction. Somehow he'd wandered off course, and now he found himself in a neighborhood he'd never seen before, a lonely place of warehouses and abandoned tenements, of ramshackle wooden firetraps and ancient factory loft buildings where, by day, illegal im-

migrants toiled in sweatshops for less than minimum wage.

At night these mean streets and midnight
alleys belonged to the homeless, to faceless men
and women whose lives were hopelessly entang-
led in cheap alcohol, toxic drugs, mental illness,
the impossibility of coping with daily life. Here
they huddled in doorways, or slept fitfully on
subway gratings from which came occasional
bursts of warm, fetid air to keep their pathetic
bones from freezing in the late October night.
Here newspaper took the place of clothing and
cardboard boxes served as shelter.

Shivering, Nelson wrapped his long flowing
coat more tightly around himself and quickened
his pace. The streets were still wet from the rain.
They gave off reflections from the street lamps,
distorted mirror images of horrible, nameless
things.

Nelson's newly-heightened senses recoiled
from the stink of garbage and unwashed bodies
and worse. Under it all, he could smell rat-
stench, stale blood and ordure, and his gorge
began to rise. He was nearly running now, but
he had to run a grotesque gauntlet. Fires were
burning in a line of garbage cans, and skeletal
humans wrapped in rags were warming their
pathetic selves by their heat. Their faces, lit from
below in the red glow of the flames, seemed to
Nelson to be grimacing death's-heads, winking
and nodding to him in ghastly conspiracy as he
raced by them.

Suddenly afraid, Nelson turned down an empty alley, hearing the pounding of his steps on the broken pavement like drumbeats in his ears, feeling the pounding of his heart like a series of massive implosions in his chest. His breath came with difficulty, rasping painfully in his throat. He had no idea what was making him so afraid. But at last he was away from those druggies, bag ladies and psychos.

He was alone. And he was lost.

Maybe he had been down these streets before, but never alone and never at night. No signposts were familiar, and the buildings appeared somehow menacing and imbued with life. Suddenly disoriented, Nelson ran down the alley, looking for a thoroughfare that would lead him to his familiar route home. But the alley twisted and narrowed, opening into a longer, even narrower alley. He stopped, hesitating, where the two alleyways crossed. Which way to go?

Then he heard it, faintly at first, but very soon louder and nearer. That dragging sound, that eerily familiar dragging. And the whining. Nelson held his breath.

"Champ?" he whispered. As if in answer to his call, the mongrel dog, still bandaged from its wounds, came slithering from the alley, dragging its useless hindquarters. It passed about thirty feet away from him, and disappeared from sight.

"Champ?" The word stuck in Nelson Wright's throat as if it were a stone. Although he couldn't see the dog, he could still hear its pathetic whining. He peered down the pitch-dark alley from which it had come.

Pity and horror fought for control of Nelson's thoughts. Why was the dog allowed to wander the streets? Shouldn't an injured animal be hospitalized? It needed help. He didn't want to follow it; his rational mind screamed at him silently not to follow it, to turn around and go home. Yet he found himself moving, terrified, down the alley, peering into the shadows for the animal, all rationality abandoned.

Thunder rattled the night sky. Long, rolling booms of noise that moved away slowly into the distance and then were lost.

"Champ?" The dog had vanished around the next corner. Nelson Wright was standing in front of the open doorway of a long, narrow building. Inside was blackness, but there seemed to be no other place into which the dog could have disappeared. It was moving too slowly to simply vanish in a second. It was badly hurt, and needed medical attention.

"Champ? Here pup, c'mon." Cautiously, Nelson stepped inside the building, recognizing it as an old icehouse, with very low ceilings and a cracked, damp concrete floor. It was lit only by a bare bulb of low wattage that cast long, crazy shadows on the peeling walls and dripping ceiling. Nelson moved slowly forward, a step at a time, his eyes searching the dimness for the wounded dog.

Up ahead, a small figure was half-hidden in the shadows. Nelson noticed it and it struck him as curious. What was a kid that young doing in a place like this at this time of night? He couldn't be more than eight or nine years old, a small thin boy in a red, hooded sweatshirt, with a sweet, sad, forlorn expression. Didn't he have a home?

"What's up, kid?" Nelson called out. "What are you doing here?" He moved closer.

The child didn't answer, but simply stood looking at Nelson, and his small face was a study in sadness. Moved, Nelson came closer still, near enough to almost count the freckles. If only the light weren't so dim . . .

"Are you lost?" he asked. "Hey kid, are you okay?"

The boy said nothing, but peered silently upward into Nelson's face. In the ghostly light, his face was alarmingly white. The dim light from the single bulb playing on it made it look all at once grotesque, like the face of a mad-dened dwarf. Without warning, the boy kicked out suddenly, and his sneakered foot caught Nelson hard in the crotch, sending him writhing to the ground.

As he lay there, clutching at himself in pain, the little boy began to beat him, his small fists as powerful as a boxer's. Smashing, merciless blows rained down on Nelson's unprotected head, the soft parts of his belly, kidneys and spleen.

Screaming an astonished protest, Nelson at-

115

tempted to protect himself or to rise to his feet, but the boy's fists were everywhere, and stronger than the strongest man's. Punches to the temple, to the jaw, to the nose, to the eyes—

"Stop it," Nelson cried in anguish, unwilling and unable to believe that this could actually be happening to him. A nine-year-old kid was beating the shit out of him, without a sound and apparently without effort. He raised his head, trying to shake the blood out of his eyes, but a hard fist caught him square on his left cheekbone next to the eye, sending Nelson toppling backward; his head slammed hard on the cold concrete floor, and everything started to swim.

Desperately clinging to the remnants of consciousness, Nelson saw the little boy standing over him, staring at him blankly, without emotion. That was the spookiest thing of all—there was no emotion in the boy's blank face, no anger in those empty eyes, eyes as empty as the wounded dog's—yet, as with the dog, there was something in the face that struck Nelson Wright as terribly, terribly familiar.

Instinctively, Nelson curled himself up in a defensive ball, his arms thrown over his head, waiting for the final destructive blows to come crashing down on him. Fatal blows; the boy was going to beat him to death. He knew it. He was helpless, thoroughly frightened and completely at the mercy of this small, dreadful boy.

But no more blows were struck. Without a word, the child turned suddenly and ran away, off into the deepest shadows of the icehouse, leaving Nelson Wright to lie on the concrete and shiver, coughing and choking on his own blood.

He caught up with her in front of the Admin building, just as she was about to enter. "Hi, I'm Joe Hurley. You're Terry, right?"

Terry Saunders, the pretty blond co-ed from Rachel Mannus's hospital group, looked up sideways at the tall, handsome young man with the smiling Irish eyes. "Uh-huh," she said.

"I heard you had a near-death experience."

Terry's smile vanished, she stiffened and began to move swiftly away. "I don't want to talk about it," she said in a tight voice.

Joe lengthened his stride and caught up with her again, in the hallway. "Wait a minute," he told her urgently. "I had a near-death experience also."

The girl stopped and looked at him doubtfully. Was he scamming, coming on to her or what? "You did?" she asked him with one eyebrow upraised.

A thousand watts of Gaelic charm poured over her like melting butter on a waffle. "I did, I really did. And I need someone to talk to. Terry, this thing changed my life." Good old Joe; who else could turn a perilous scientific experiment into a guaranteed pussy-trap?

Terry stopped, obviously torn, which gave Joe the chance to scope out her bod; he was one of those rare men who can look deeply into a woman's eyes and assess her bra size at the same time. "Just have coffee with me," he pleaded, knowing that Terry would not, could not, say no.

The two of them entered the student lounge, which had been recently decorated for Hallowe'en, with shocks of cornstalks propped up in the corners of the room, and a real pumpkin on every table. Joe went to get two cups of coffee, not noticing that a couple of girls were shooting him angry looks, and standing up to walk out when they saw him. Seduced and abandoned, and furious about it.

Terry was sitting demurely at a table, her legs crossed under her pleated skirt, and Joe ran his eyes over her body again as he set the cups down. Definitely screenworthy. He made a mental note to buy some more blank videotapes right away; his last few tapes had been used up in the Dog Lab experiments.

Grinning charmingly, he set the cups down, and Terry, encouraged by his interest, couldn't wait to get started on the narration of her near-death experience.

"Well, first of all, they didn't even believe me."

Joe leaned supportively over the table. "Well, we were there, right?" he said huskily. "We know."

"I'll never forget it," she began, but Joe put his hand gently on her arm and stopped her.

"I want to hear everything," he said with false sincerity. "But if you have to go to class, well, maybe we could grab a bite some night this week and compare notes."

But Terry was on a roll and there was no

stopping her now. "You know, all that day I knew that something was going to happen," she confided. "I've always had premonitions about things. Once, my aunt was supposed to fly in from Las Vegas? You know? And I said to my mother, I said—"

Joe Hurley was only pretending to listen; part of his attention was aimed at the blonde who was babbling away, while the rest of it idly scanned the student lounge, coming to rest on the TV set that sat on the back wall. It was playing, of course; the student lounge TV was never switched off. When they'd sat down, Joe had noticed that a college football game was on the air.

Suddenly, all of Joe's attention became glued to the small screen. Could that be a porno tape? A fuck film, here, in the Admin? Certainly looked like one. Definitely yes. There was a man and a woman making it, and now the girl's face was turned toward the camera and . . .

Holy shit! It was impossible! The girl was Barbara Mullins, the man was himself, and the tape was one of the sex tapes from Joe Hurley's secret cabinet! How the hell could it be? Who stole the fuckin' tape?

Oddly enough, nobody else seemed to be paying attention to the naked girl writhing under the man's body; nobody but Joe was watching the screen. And now the girl in the videotape turned her face to Joe; her eyes looked straight into his.

"Why'd you do this to me, Joe?" she asked.

Joe turned white. With a scream and a curse, he leaped to his feet, knocking his chair over in his scramble to get away. What the hell was going on here? He ran from the lounge, heedless of Terry staring after him indignantly, heedless of the puzzled looks and muffled laughter of the other students. All he could see was Barbara's reproachful face, all he could hear was Barbara's sad voice, all he could think of was that this was not fuckin' happening; this could not be fuckin' happening.

Nelson Wright locked his apartment door behind him. With all his strength he held on to consciousness, even though his battered body was crying out for oblivion. He almost hadn't made it up the stairs of his old apartment building. Out of breath, he moved slowly on trembling legs to his bathroom, where he ran warm water into the sink and gingerly bathed the cuts and bruises on his face. They hurt like hell, and hurt even worse when Nelson applied the antiseptic.

In the glaring white light of his spotless bathroom, Nelson took a blurry look at himself in the mirror, and it made him nearly puke. He looked like hamburger meat, like ten pounds of shit in a five-pound sack. Both his eyelids were swollen, the left one nearly swollen shut. The cut above his cheekbone near his left eye would not stop bleeding; it was large and deep, and would require stitching.

Opening his medicine cabinet, Nelson took out a needle and some surgical ligature. Keeping his hand steady was no small achievement, given his condition, but he managed to sew the cut closed. The pain was excruciating. Now he wanted nothing out of life more than a hot shower and his bed. He was desperate for sleep, both his body and his mind crying out for rest.

It was then he heard the footsteps.

They were coming closer, closer to the front door of his apartment. They were a child's footsteps, and they were just outside the door.

Don't answer it, his body pleaded. Stay away from the door. Even so, against his will, Nelson found himself going to the front door of his apartment. He pressed his ear against the wood and listened. His mind was dizzy with fear and his pulses were racing with deadly apprehension.

Nothing.

Nelson looked down at the opaque glass panel that was set into the door near the bottom of the frame. With a gasp of fright, he shrank away. Through the glass he could see the blurry outline of two small feet. A little boy's feet.

Throwing himself back from the door, Nelson cringed against the wall. He was sweating and shivering at the same time, and small moans escaped his lips without his hearing them. Under his torn and bloody shirt, his heart was pounding rapidly, and though his palms were wet, his mouth was very dry.

He had to get out of here. Now.

Racing through his apartment to the kitchen, Nelson grabbed a coat off a hook, and flung himself almost bodily through the back door. His exhaustion had been obliterated by the adrenaline of fear that pumped octane through his veins. The only thing in his mind was that he had to get away. Taking the back steps two and three at a time, he hurled himself down the rear staircase and threw open the fire door that led to the ground floor landing.

Nelson looked out cautiously. Nobody was in the lobby. It was empty. Good. He stepped out of the doorway, onto the cold marble floor of the old building's ornate lobby. Then he heard the footsteps, the light footsteps, the child's footsteps. They were coming down the front stairs. They were coming down into the lobby.

Nelson turned back; he grabbed the fire door handle and twisted it desperately. No use. The fire door opened only from the inside; now that he was in the lobby, it was firmly locked. He was trapped.

"Shit, no!" he cried out.

Hyperventilating, he pressed himself up against the wall, hoping to disappear into the shadows. The footsteps were coming down from the second floor now. Nearer and nearer. Now they reached the lobby. From his hiding place, Nelson could see a small form crossing the lobby, coming straight toward him. A child's form. He could only stand there paralyzed, cringing, waiting, choking on a fear so strong and bitter he could taste it like bile in his throat.

"Trick or treat!"

The two little girls in Hallowe'en costumes lived on the third floor; the smaller one came to stand in front of Nelson holding out her dime-store goodie bag printed all over with black cats and pumpkins. The sight of her made his heart stop, and he pushed past her, running swiftly into the cold night.

Jesus Christ, what the hell is happening to me?

It had to have been some kind of hallucination, thought Joe Hurley as he put on his Hallowe'en costume, a black body stocking with a glow-in-the-dark skeleton screen-printed on it. Probably some reaction to all those damn drugs they'd pumped into him while he was on the gurney. A flashback, maybe, like some stupid acid trip. A momentary craziness, oxygen deprivation, definitely a hallucination. He absolutely positively did not see himself and Barbara Mullins fucking on the student lounge television set, or hear her call out to him. The "Barbara" tape was still safely tucked away in his cabinet. He'd checked it first thing, the minute he got home.

So there was no reason to freak out. Everything was cool; tonight was Labraccio's turn on the hot seat. Meanwhile, party, party, party. It was Hallowe'en, right? The Delts were throwing a big costume bash, and yours truly was urgently requested to be there. With bones on.

There were goblins and ghouls and beasties and witches at the party, and any number of them were female and available. Hurley felt terrific, on top of the world. Why not? He'd been there and back, had returned safely, and was hardly expected to go again. Tonight he'd pick off one of these beauties and get himself laid; there was a fresh tape in the camcorder, and—

"Shit!" The camcorder. Tonight at the Dog Lab. David Labraccio was in the box. Joe glanced at his watch. Eight-thirty. He not only didn't have time to make out, he didn't even have time to go home and change out of this skeleton suit. He pushed his way through all that willing flesh, squeezing past luscious asses and bobbing tits, and made his way to the dorm door, and out into the hallway.

Above his head in the hallway was a black-and-white security monitor, one of those setups that scans every floor to make certain there are no unwarranted intruders. Only now, on the monitor, instead of seeing doors and elevators, Joe saw Marcia Monaghan, exactly as she was when he was filming her, naked and thrashing in the hot throes of sex with Joe Hurley.

Shit, no!

Marcia turned her head so that she was looking straight at Joe, and her face crumpled a little in sorrow. She reached one hand up, almost as though she were pointing at him.

"I trusted you, Joe," she said, directly into the

camera. "I trusted you."

With a terrified yip, Joe ran pell-mell down the hallway and out the front door, running, running, to get away from that face on the screen, that hand, that voice.

Jesus Christ, what the hell is happening to me?

CHAPTER 8

Hallowe'en night. Outside the Dog Lab, in the real world, under a round full orange moon, macabre celebrations were beginning, their origins lost in pagan antiquity. Little children ran from house to house like mischievous goblins, their deviltry appeased only by sacrifices of Snickers bars. Their costumes of skeletons, ghosts and witches invoked the racial memory of that ancient spirit-haunted night before All Saints' Day, the night when graves yawned wide to surrender their dead, when Satan himself rose up from his dominions below to dance and copulate with his eager covens. Every secret sacred thing that the coming of Christianity stamped out ruthlessly long ago came flowing back through the cracks in hidden places on this one night of the year.

On the campus, the orgiastic *Walpurgisnacht* was already under way. The quadrangle had come alive, teeming with all manner of monster. Every year, the undergraduates vied with one another to see who could come up with the wildest costume, and every year there was more than one winner. Grim-faced devils boogied down with busty whores in black mesh stockings. Two-headed animals draped in sheets danced crazily around the huge bonfire, while raucous rock-and-roll music made tatters of the night air.

In the dimly-lit heart of the deserted Taft building, inside the Dog Lab with shades drawn, Rachel, Steckle and Labraccio were busy setting up for David's impending trip. David had already stripped to the waist and was sitting on the edge of the gurney. They were getting a little antsy. So far, they hadn't heard a word from either Nelson or Joe, and it was getting past time. Weren't they coming?

"I don't know, you guys," said Steckle nervously. "It's Hallowe'en, a full moon. Don't you think we might be pushing this just a little bit?"

David Labraccio smiled. He was outwardly calm, but inwardly riddled with anxieties, just as Nelson and Joe had been in their turn. Here he sat, about to put his life into the hands of amateurs, promising to remain dead longer than any had before him. And for what? To stop Rachel from going? To prove a point? What

point? That it was all stupid, that it should stop?
Wasn't he perpetuating Nelson's fantasy by vol-
unteering to be the next guinea pig? And
shouldn't he admit, at least to himself, that
underneath all his skepticism he was curious,
intrigued by the possibility that, just maybe,
Nelson was right, and there was something out
there. But even if there were, why couldn't he
wait sixty years or so to find out?

What if they lost him? What if they weren't
able to bring him back? Then he'd never climb
K-2, or Annapurna or Mt. Everest, never find the
cure for anything, never heal anybody or save a
life, never love and marry and bring children
into this world. The world would have to muddle
along without David Labraccio.

So be it, then. David's rational mind never
attempted to place an ordered structure on a
random universe; to him, life was a momentary
and soon-forgotten eyeblink of eternity. There
was no God, no Maker, no deeper purpose to
creation than its re-creation and procreation.
Well, that was good enough for Dave. Someday
the planet would go back to the insects, and that
was okay with him, too.

"Sorry I'm late."

There was a movement at the door, and the
three of them turned nervously. They recognized Nelson Wright, although they couldn't see
his face until he came forward into the light of
the high-beam work lamps. When they saw it,
they gasped. He'd been beaten, beaten badly.

"Nelson? What happened?" David slipped off

the gurney and took a step forward, but Nelson waved him off with a stiff, painful grimace that barely resembled his old smile. "Does it look as bad as it feels?" he joked feebly.

"It does," Steckle assured him.

"Who did it?" Rachel wanted to know.

Nelson shrugged dismissively. The action made him wince in pain. "Some guys, big guys. I didn't know 'em. It doesn't matter."

Another rustle at the doorway and the Flatliners turned to see, floating into the lab, a glowing skeleton. Rachel Mannus uttered a stifled scream. Nelson turned pale and Steckle jumped. But it was only Joe Hurley in his Hallowe'en costume. Joe wore a flowing black cloak, and underneath it a body stocking of deep black that melted into the darkness, screened with a phosphorescent skeleton that glowed eerily in the dark.

"Where the hell have you been?" Randy Steckle demanded.

"I don't feel very well," said Joe, and in truth he didn't look well; he appeared subdued and distracted. "What the hell happened to you?" he gasped as he saw Nelson's battered features and the freshly-sutured cut on his face.

"Enough. Don't worry about me, worry about your camera."

"Nice outfit," Labraccio joked to Joe, trying to relieve some of his own nervousness.

"Yeah, who are you supposed to be, Boner-Man?" Steckle needled sarcastically.

"You ready?" Nelson Wright asked. His face was intent, serious.

David nodded. "Ready."

There was no reason to delay now; all the Flatliners were here. Labraccio sat down on the gurney, and Rachel attached the EKG electrodes to his bare chest. Under her hands she could feel the rapid pounding of his heart belying his appearance of cool.

"Think about a place that's nice," she murmured to him, her long fingers barely touching David's chest. "It'll help you to relax." She smiled at him reassuringly.

David smiled back at her, and Nelson, noticing the exchange, felt a sudden sharp pain behind his eyes. Randy Steckle attached the EEG leads to Labraccio's skull, while Hurley checked the battery pack of his camcorder. Everything was now in standby readiness; Rachel picked up the syringe with the sodium pentothal injection.

"Two twenty. Don't forget," said Labraccio.

"Hurry back," Nelson answered. "You can buy us breakfast."

"Nelson." Labraccio smiled, and his eyes met his friend's eyes. "Don't let go of the rope."

And then Nelson pushed twenty cc's of sodium pentothal into the IV, Steckle placed the nitrous oxide mask over Labraccio's face, and David set off on his journey.

There's an ancient belief that when a person drowns, his entire life flashes before his eyes.

131

David Labraccio didn't feel as though he were drowning; in fact, air seemed to fill his lungs almost to the breaking point. Pure, clean air, not the dirty polluted effluence of cities. It was air like the air he'd breathed only on mountaintops. Yet, there was his entire life, rushing past him (or was he rushing past it?) in a series of dizzying flashbacks.

David saw himself walking and talking with Rachel, only an hour ago. He watched himself running his daily six-miler; hammering his pitons into a cliff side on his way up the face of a mountain; shooting baskets. He saw himself reaching into that dying woman's entrails to connect her severed artery; bicycle racing . . . wait! He hadn't raced a bicycle since high school! But now he saw his old high school, and his friends from grammar school, and the little town in Illinois he called home, with its Fourth of July parades and its marching band. Image after image from his life flashed by him at dizzying speed. He wanted to reach out to all of them, to embrace them, but he was moving too quickly, flying toward the crests of the mountain range that waited only for him up ahead.

Yes, it was he who was flying, he who was moving so quickly, soaring, feeling so free, his lungs so bright with the purity of the air. . . . It was exactly like climbing a mountain, except there was no effort at all. And now he was above the crests of those snow-topped mountains he'd never seen before, except in his imagination.

Were they the Alps? The Himalayas? The Rockies? He didn't know, but they were so beautiful and untouched they made him want to weep with joy. Everything that ever happened to him in his life was spread out below.

"Flatline," announced Joe, lensing the EKG monitor.

Steckle took the oxygen mask off David's face, all the while speaking into his little recorder. "As I remove the oxygen mask, my hands tremble slightly," he intoned dramatically.

"Shut up, Steckle," growled Nelson, shutting the monitor's tone off. The Flatliners watched anxiously as the EEG needles recorded the progress of David Labraccio's brain death. Flatter and flatter, until the lines went straight across the screen. Rachel looked at her watch, making note of the exact second that they flatlined.

Flatline.

"What if he didn't make it?" Nelson asked Rachel in a low voice. He glanced slyly at her. "Would you miss him?"

The girl didn't answer, but Nelson could see a flicker of contempt cross her face. And something more. Unhappiness, perhaps? Fear for David Labraccio's life?

"One minute," Steckle told his recorder.

He could hear a kind of singing; sweet children's voices, little girls' voices, drifting over the mountains, but he couldn't make out the words. No, it wasn't exactly singing. More like chanting, the same words over and over again. What were they chanting? Why couldn't he make out the words?

"Two minutes," Steckle spoke into the mini-recorder. "Over twice the time of our first venture into the beyond."

Hurley aimed his camera at the monitors, and gasped. There should have been only flatlines up there on the screens. Instead, he saw himself naked with another of his women, having sex. Appalled, he looked around him. Didn't any of the others see? No, they appeared to be entirely absorbed in the experiment. But any minute now, one of them could be checking the monitors and would see the tape. Then his humiliation would be total. He sidled crabwise toward the monitors, and stood between them and the Flatliners, trying to block the screens from view.

He could see the little girls now, and they were about ten years old, in a playground waiting their turn to jump rope. They were clapping their hands in time to the chant, while two of them turned the jump rope for Double Dutch, and two more jumped in and out of the ropes with incredible precision. It was a jumping rhyme the girls were chanting, the kind of children's playparty chant that comes down through the centuries, an oral tradition. The rope-jumping made him feel uneasy. Yet, why should a simple children's game, unchanged for five hundred years and more, make him uneasy?

"Ninety degrees. Stations," called Rachel. Steckle and Nelson took up their positions, Randy at the refrigerated blanket and Nelson by the defibrillator paddles. They worked fairly efficiently together, but all the while the dark shadow on Nelson Wright's soul was growing.

"What do you say we give him another five seconds?" he suggested slyly to Rachel.

"What?" The girl turned to him dumbfounded, and her moth-wing brows were raised in astonishment.

"Or ten? Why not? Why not ten? We have a little more time to decide."

"Stations, Joe," snapped Rachel. "You're blocking our view." She'd deal with Nelson Wright later, after Labraccio was back. At this moment, she had other priorities. They had a life to save.

"C'mon," scowled Steckle nervously. "No kidding around here. Two fifteen."

"Ninety-two degrees," said Rachel, concentrating fiercely.

Only seconds to resuscitation, and the Dog Lab was electric with tension, the atmosphere as highly charged as the defib paddles. Joe Hurley backed uncomfortably away from the monitors, hoping that the others would be too absorbed in their work to notice his fuck tape, unrolling crazily on the screen. He realized suddenly that something was different. While he'd been worrying about the tape, there'd been some change in the dynamics of the group.

"Wh . . . What's going on here?" he mumbled.

"Quiet!" barked Rachel Mannus. Somehow, she was now in charge, and Nelson was following orders. Her face was grim and determined, her wide mouth set in a thin line, and she never took her eyes off the unmoving body of David Labraccio.

Steckle began the final countdown. "Fifteen, sixteen, seventeen—"

Snap! A sudden loud noise at the window made them all start in surprise. Joe yelled "Damn it!" and Randy Steckle let out a muffled yip. They turned and froze.

The window shade flew up, revealing ghastly faces at the window, dead souls, ghouls from hell. It took them a second to realize that it was only a group of undergraduates in Hallowe'en masks. But until they did, precious seconds were wasted. Joe rushed angrily to the window and yanked the shade back down.

"Two minutes twenty seconds," announced Rachel. She turned to Nelson Wright, who was rubbing the defibrillator paddles together to charge them. "Hand them over," she snapped. Rachel no longer had faith in Nelson Wright, and what's more, she didn't trust him. Something about him was . . . unwholesome.

But Nelson held tightly onto the defib paddles.

"This is my lab," he snapped back. "Three hundred joules. Charged. Clear." He zapped Labraccio hard with the paddles.

He wasn't on top of the mountains anymore. He was roaring through a tunnel, maybe some kind of train? He wasn't clear on that. It was dark, and he couldn't see anything, yet oddly enough he could still hear the slap of the jump rope and the chanting of the little girls, the rhythmic clapping of their hands as they kept time with the turning ropes. And now a face was coming toward him from the darkness. One face. One small black girl's face.

"Sodium bicarb and eppy in," called Rachel.

Dave wasn't breathing. They'd been working on him for almost a minute, but there was still no sign of life. They stepped up the code.

"Three-one-thousand, four-one-thousand, five-one-thousand, what comes next?" It was a feeble joke, but Nelson was sweating as Rachel worked over Labraccio's body, her hands pumping hard at Dave's chest.

"Five-one-thousand, breathe!" Nelson snatched up the defibrillator paddles and charged them up. "Two hundred joules! Charge! Clear!"

Current coursed through Labraccio's body, and the heart monitor uttered a tiny feeble blip.

"That's it! That's it!" Randy Steckle yelled.

"That's not it," barked Rachel, and she was

right. Flatline again. No action from David Labraccio's heart. "Charge them again. Three-hundred."

"Atropine," offered Steckle.

"Not yet," snapped Rachel. Her hair had come loose over her brow and was plastered down by sweat. "Clear!" She zapped David once more, but the EKG monitor still flatlined. "Increase defib paddles to three-fifty. Charge. Clear!"

Nothing.

Nothing was happening. Not the smallest glimmer of life. Labraccio had been right. This whole experiment had been crazy from beginning to end. They'd all been crazy. Two minutes and twenty seconds—madness! Dave had told them it was too dangerous, that they should stop before it was too late. They should have listened to his warning. How ironic that it should be David Labraccio for whom it would be too late.

"Three minutes!" yelled Steckle, close to hysteria. "He's been under too long." Rachel remained terribly focused.

"Starting CPR again," Nelson announced, as he began to work on Labraccio's chest. "Joe, keep filming. One-one-thousand, two-one-thousand."

Joe Hurley picked up his camcorder and held the viewfinder to his eye. But, instead of the body of David Labraccio, he saw a woman's naked body, a woman's face turned toward him in reproach, and he heard a woman's voice.

"You lied to me, Joe," it said sorrowfully.

Uttering a muffled cry, he almost dropped the camera, but managed barely, by the tips of his fingers, to hold onto it. What were these hallucinations? Why was he being haunted this way? Was he losing his mind? Was he going nuts?

"Lidocaine, push!" called Rachel, as she slipped the syringe into David's IV. And still no response.

"Somebody do something," moaned Steckle miserably.

A kind of electricity coursed through all of them; it was as though they were connected to one another and to David by the EEG leads and the EKG electrodes fastened to David Labraccio's head and body. They'd tried everything—the stimulants, the CPR, the defib paddles, and so far none of it had worked. Labraccio was dead and he was going to stay dead. The panic in the Dog Lab was real enough to taste, and the taste was bitter. It was the bitter taste of three minutes and fifty seconds.

"Nelson, three-sixty!" yelled Rachel.

Charging the paddles up to three hundred and sixty joules, Nelson Wright rubbed them together, yelled "Clear!" and slammed them hard against Labraccio's motionless body.

Blip!

All at once, the EKG beeped strongly, and a magical little heart appeared on the monitor, followed by a set of lines that peaked. For an instant of eternity, the four of them froze, staring at the monitor, willing it to beep again.

Blip! And it did, a series of electronic signals now, strong and steady, like the beat of David Labraccio's living heart. Both monitors were working now, busily charting signs that were vital again. David Labraccio was starting back from his journey into death.

"O-2, stand by," called Rachel.

"Got him!" Joe yelled.

"One milligram of epinephrine, in!" Nelson shoved the stimulant into the IV.

That was it, that was really it this time. They got him. They hadn't let go of the rope. Dave was alive. They all grinned at one another in sheer relief.

"Never again," thought Joe, and his hands trembled as he focused the video camera on Dave's living face. "I'm never going through with this again."

"Oh boy," whimpered Randy Steckle. "Oh, my God. That was close. That was very close. That was too damn close."

"Thank you, God," thought Rachel gratefully. "Thank you, dear sweet Lord Jesus."

With the defib paddles still in his hands, Nelson slumped back against the wall. Now, suddenly, he could breathe.

When Labraccio had been taken home and tucked into his bed, when he'd recovered some of his strength, and had ingested some fluids, the Flatliners gathered around him to hear what he had to tell them. David's account, coming from the atheist who always expressed strong doubts about an afterlife, was the one they really wanted to hear.

"What did you say back there?" asked Joe.

"It's a war cry of the Sioux Indians. Very macho. It means 'Today—'"

"Today is a good day to die," finished Nelson. He knew that Labraccio had seen something, had experienced something. This was Nelson's personal moment of triumph, the conversion of the skeptic.

"Was it, Dave? Was it a good day to die?"

But David wasn't ready to convert so easily. He shook his head weakly. "I don't know if I was dead. It was something . . . I don't know . . . like a dream, or some stuff stored up inside my mind—"

But Nelson Wright wasn't buying any of that. "You were brain-dead, Labraish." He smiled. "There was no mind."

"Yeah, but electrical current still circulating through the body—"

"Would have shown up on the EEG monitor. David, you were dead. So why don't you just tell us what happened?"

Labraccio looked around at the rest of them. Steckle was holding his little Sony up to David's lips, to catch his every syllable. Joe was listening eagerly, and Nelson wore that glittery smile of his. As for Rachel, she said nothing, but her eyes were intent on his face, and David Labraccio could read her questions in her eyes.

"It's hard to verbalize," he began slowly. "It's like being paranoid without the fear, like you're being watched."

Nelson's eyes flickered briefly, and Hurley gave a small start, but David Labraccio didn't notice. "I don't know. It was probably just you guys standing over me."

"What do you mean? Who could be watching?" Steckle asked.

"The dead," Nelson said softly.

"I didn't say that," Labraccio objected.

"But the skeptic did feel something, didn't ya?" Triumph made Nelson Wright's eyes glitter, and two spots of color rose into his pale cheeks. "I'm going again," he announced.

Rachel Mannus stood up angrily. "No way, Nelson. I've been bumped twice."

But Nelson was possessed now, caught up in something he couldn't stop and wouldn't change. "The bidding starts at four minutes," he announced.

A stunned silence followed his words. Then Rachel gasped, "Four minutes?" It was an inconceivably long stretch of time.

"Labraccio went for three fifty," Nelson pointed out, still wearing that crazy smile.

"But that was a mistake!" Steckle squeaked in protest.

"Anything less than four minutes would be redundant now," Nelson said coldly.

Randy shook his head. "Nobody's going for four minutes."

FLATLINERS

"Nobody's going at all," snapped Labraccio.

"Four twenty-five," said Rachel quietly. Her dark eyes burned with her intensity, and she met their stunned stares with a stubborn lift of her chin. "I'm next, or I'm out for good."

"Without Rachel's help, five minutes will be hard enough, but without me—" Labraccio said softly.

"Or me," put in Randy Steckle, but Joe Hurley said nothing.

Nelson Wright took a long drag on his cigarette, and his green eyes narrowed, although the icy smile never left his lips.

"Well, mutiny at last." Then anger blazed across his face and for the first time he raised his voice. "You know, I trusted you with an idea so simple, so brilliant that you get one in a lifetime."

"Why don't you give it a rest, Nelson?" Labraccio put in.

Nelson whirled furiously. "No, you give it a rest," he said in a harsh tone, and his face was so pale that the fresh cut on his cheekbone stood out an angry red. "None of you had the foresight or the balls to do any of this until *I* did it. Rachel, you wanna go next? Well, be my guest. Fuck the rest of you! This is *my* idea. You're just tourists."

With those angry words, he stormed out of David's apartment, slamming the door behind him, leaving the others speechless.

* * *

"I might have gone three thirty, or maybe three forty . . . I'm not saying I would," lied Steckle as he and Hurley walked home together from Labraccio's. Randy had no intention of getting dead at all, let alone staying dead for more than three minutes. "But four twenty-five is crazy. We're pushing the five-minute mark here. Dangerous. Zucchini land. At this point, I really have to question Nelson's judgment—"

But Joe Hurley had stopped hearing Steckle's babble. They were walking on the avenue past a home appliance store, and the window had a display of television sets, all of which had been tuned to one program.

To Joe's sex tapes.

Face after face was turned to him, women's eyes probed into his soul, women's voices—sad, accusing—clashed like cymbals in his ears.

"You said you loved me, Joe."

"I trusted you, Joe."

"Why did you do this to me, Joe?"

"Why, Joe, why?"

"You're a shit, Joe."

And suddenly, Anne's face, Anne's voice. "I love you, Joe."

He shut his eyes, but he couldn't shut out the faces. He closed his ears, but he still heard the voices. They were inside him, outside of him, all around him. They gave him no peace. Like the Furies, they wouldn't let him rest. They would go on haunting him for the rest of his—

"Skeletor?" Randall Steckle was tugging at his arm. "Hurley, you listening to me?"

Anger and resentment dogged Nelson Wright's footsteps all the way home. The ingratitude of them! He'd offered them everything on a plate—fame, the opportunity to make the most important discovery in the history of science—and what had they given him in return? They'd turned on him like ungrateful dogs, snapping at his outstretched hand.

Labraccio was the worst of them. He was my friend. At least, I thought he was. But once he'd got a sniff of Mannus, friendship went out the fuckin' window. The two of them playing footsie, making eye contact, keeping their little secrets. Well, fuck them! Fuck them all! He could do without any one of them. Steckle and Hurley, too.

Letting himself into his sparsely-furnished apartment, Nelson took his coat off and hung it on a rack near the door. He was beat, ready for bed. He walked into his bedroom and froze in horror.

There, on his pristine white sheets, were the muddy prints of a little boy's sneakers. A print on his pillowcase, too, mocking him, saying to him, "Nothing is safe, Nelson. Nothing is safe from me. Not even your own white bed. Not even the place where you close your eyes at night."

He spun around, his eyes searching the room,

145

afraid of what he would find, knowing what that would be.

Oh, he was there all right, the little boy in the red, hooded sweatshirt. The silent little boy with the evil little face. In his hand he was holding Nelson's hockey stick and, before Nelson could protect himself, the boy swung it hard, cracking it across his unprotected chest and belly.

With a groan of anguish, Nelson fell to his knees, and the boy went on hitting him with the stick across his back, breaking the hockey stick in two.

Nelson struggled to his feet, but the boy was on him like a spider monkey, all agile arms and legs, and powerfully strong. Staggering, Nelson fell backward on the bed, and the boy knelt on his chest, pinning him down, not letting him move. He was terribly heavy, like a leaden weight on Nelson's heart.

Up to this moment, Nelson Wright could not admit to himself that he knew this child, he knew his face and he knew his name. But now he couldn't keep the recognition out of his mind. Billy Mahoney. The little boy in the red, hooded sweatshirt was Billy Mahoney.

And now the little boy Billy Mahoney smiled, a dreadful smile, a smile from hell. Slowly, he opened his mouth, showing Nelson a ball of spit beginning to form. Then he allowed the dribble of spit to drool slowly down, towards Nelson's face. Before it touched the skin, the little boy in

the red, hooded sweatshirt sucked it back up. He
did it again. And again. Then he spat.

And Nelson Wright began to scream. . . .

CHAPTER 9

Labraccio woke up with the taste of pennies in his mouth, a powerful thirst, and an unspeakable headache, pain like nails being pounded into his skull by Thor's hammer. For a moment or two, he wasn't sure where he was, but when he looked up and saw the monumental poster of the Himalayan mountains he'd tacked up over his bed three years ago when he started med school, he knew he was safely back in his own bedroom.

And he wasn't alone. Incredibly, the beautiful Rachel Mannus was with him. She was standing across the room, near the window, folding a blanket. Light from the window drew a nimbus of radiance around her, outlining her head and her long, slender body. She looked incredible. She'd spent the night curled up in a chair under that blanket, watching over him, making certain he was all right. David felt a sudden powerful surge of emotion toward her that left him drained.

"Hey, thanks for stayin'," he called out softly.

Rachel pushed her long hair out of her eyes. She looked tired, which made her appear younger, little more than a girl. She gave Labraccio a smile. "I'm on early shift at the hospital. You seem fine. So I'll see you later."

"Later" was a word that held a world of meaning between them. "Later" meant the Dog Lab, the gurney, the refrigerated blanket, the sodium pentothal, and that perilous journey into death. "Later" meant flatline for Rachel.

"Wait a minute." David climbed out of bed, and reached for his robe. "About tonight—"

"Don't try to talk me out of it," Rachel said.

"Why you doin' this?" He came closer to her, close enough to touch her, but no matter how much he wanted to touch her—and it was a great deal of wanting—he knew better.

The girl drew a deep breath, and turned her lovely solemn face to his. She spoke slowly, intently, as though the words were being pulled out of her by force.

"Look, people who were close to me have died. I just want to make sure they've gone to a good place. Does that sound trivial?" Her dark eyes supplicated his.

Labraccio shook his head. "No, to tell you the

truth, that's the only good reason I've heard so far. Listen to me, Rachel. There's something I didn't tell you about last night. . . ." He groped for words. "I . . . had this feeling that if I had gone a little farther, there was . . . something out there . . . protecting me. You know? Something . . ."

"Good," finished Rachel, and David nodded, even though "good" wasn't really the word he would have used to describe it.

"So you don't need to go under," he finished.

Rachel smiled suddenly, a wide, warm smile that lit up her face and made her beauty suddenly incandescent. "You're trying to tell me that the atheist now believes in God?" she teased him.

Labraccio looked deeply into her eyes. "I'm tryin' to tell you that I don't want you to do it."

For the first time, Rachel Mannus didn't turn away from Labraccio's intensity. It seemed to him that she understood everything he was trying to tell her, including the subtext he wasn't sure he understood himself. Even so, she was not to be dissuaded.

"Just think of all we'll have to talk about when you bring me back," she said lightly.

And then she was out the door, and for the next hour all David Labraccio could do was brood, letting his feelings eat away at him. Until "later."

Rachel moved around the ward almost mechanically. Her body performed the menial tasks to which she was assigned, but her thoughts kept returning to tonight and what tonight would bring. It wasn't exactly fear that she felt—although it wasn't exactly not fear, either—but a kind of anxious anticipation. Tonight she would learn what Nelson, Joe and David already knew. Tonight she would journey to where they'd already been.

Four minutes and twenty-five seconds. Longer than any of them had been . . . she tried to avoid the word, but it kept recurring in her mind. Dead. Longer than any of them had been dead. Even David Labraccio had been under for only three fifty. Did it mean that she would be able to go further—to encounter face-to-face that protective Something that Dave had talked about? Or did it mean that the others wouldn't be able to bring her back? Was four twenty-five too long a time for successful resuscitation?

David. Rachel let her thoughts remain on him for a minute, recalling the laser beam of light that was his thin face with its deep hooded eyes. Clearly in her mind she saw again the way his thick, straight hair flopped over his brow, and grew so long, almost to his broad straight shoulders. She understood what he was telling her— that he cared, that he wanted her to be safe, but David had no idea what was driving her onward to go. If he had, then maybe he'd understand why she had to do it, and know too why fear couldn't stop her.

How did she feel about him? To tell the truth, mostly confused. She had always liked him, his quiet air of authority, the honesty of his gaze and his straightforward way of talking. She respected him, as a fellow medical student, as a fellow human being. But now she found herself wanting to touch the hair on his forehead, to push it out of his eyes, to caress with the tips of her fingers the skin on his prominent cheekbones. She had no time for feelings like these. At least, not until after "later."

When she reached Mrs. Ashby's bed, Rachel stopped. The dying woman always held a claim on the girl's attention and sympathy, but today was different, even more special. She sat down on the chair beside the bed, and took the old woman's hand in her cool fingers.

"I'm dying. Don't lie to me." Mrs. Ashby searched Rachel's eyes for an answer.

Always before, Rachel had told the easy lie, to make the woman feel better. You're doing fine. You'll be better soon. But today was different. Today was special. She smiled into the patient's eyes. "Sometimes we just have to let go," she said softly.

The old woman nodded. "That's what the voices say."

"What voices?" Eagerly, Rachel leaned forward to hear Mrs. Ashby's words.

"They say, 'Have you done enough? Have you told everyone you love them?' But I have . . . I have . . ." Near tears, Mrs. Ashby tossed feverishly on her pillow.

"It's okay." Rachel gently pressed the old woman's anguished hand. "They're friendly

153

voices, and they're just telling you what you need to know."

The woman turned her face up to Rachel's, her eyes pleading. "What? What are they telling me?"

"That you have someplace to go," whispered Rachel.

Tears filled Mrs. Ashby's eyes, and rolled down her wrinkled cheeks. "Do you believe that?" she quavered.

Rachel nodded. "Yes," she said firmly, happily. "I do. Yes, I do."

All day long, David Labraccio couldn't pull his thoughts away from Rachel Mannus. He felt helpless; he knew she wouldn't back down from four minutes and twenty-five seconds, and he was afraid for her. It was quite possible that they wouldn't be able to bring her back. He didn't want to see her die. He didn't want to see anybody die, but especially not Rachel. He sensed a tenderness, an unexplored vulnerability in the girl and he ached to know her much better, and for a very, very long time. There was already a strong attraction growing between them. He felt it and he believed she did, too.

He went to spend the rest of the day in an athletic field on the other side of the city, testing his condition against physical obstacles. It seemed to Labraccio, as he jogged around the cinder track for the fifth time, that his near-death experience hadn't done him any physical harm; he was a little tired, but his wind appeared to be good, and his reflexes just about back to normal. It was getting late, and he should be getting back. He'd have to take the train.

It was the tail end of rush hour. The El was crowded with passengers, commuters going home from work, jammed together in the packed cars, hanging on to straps. Each was wrapped in his own thoughts, oblivious to the presence of the other bodies around him. The train was just one last hassle in a hassle-filled day.

Now the El was heading downward, going into a tunnel. Darkness descended on the cars, punctuated by strobelike bursts of illumination as the train hurtled past the lights on the tunnel walls.

"Hey, Fellatio!" a child's voice called out.

The word was so sudden, so startling, that Labraccio turned, his eyes trying to pierce the darkness.

"Got a match?" the child's voice went on sarcastically. "Well, I do. Your face and my ass. Your breath and a buffalo fart."

Light flashed into the car, and suddenly David saw her. A little black girl, perhaps ten years old, neatly dressed, her hair in two tidy braids with ribbons on their ends. And suddenly, with a gasp of horror, David Labraccio knew two things with certainty.

First, the little girl was talking to him.

And second, she was the same little girl whose face he'd seen in his journey into death.

He looked around, and it seemed to Labraccio

that the other people in the car had heard her curse at him, and weren't shocked; rather, they were amused by the barrage of filth that came spewing out of her baby mouth.

"Do I know you?" he asked, almost afraid to hear her answer.

"You don't know jack shit, butt-wad," she snarled, and the barrage of obscene words, issuing in a stream from those innocent childish lips, seemed to carry a double impact of derision and scorn. "You needle-dick, cock-bite, jack-off, limp-wrist, corn-hole, banana-breath—"

Recoiling from the savage verbal attack, Labraccio tried to back off, get away from the child and her insults, but the train was very crowded, and he was trapped, forced to listen. It was as though his back was up against an unyielding wall. This was the single worst moment of his life. What did she want from him? And why him?

"Shit bird, bird-turd, turd-face, kiss-ass, brown-nose, macho wimp, limp-dick, fuck-face, turd-merchant . . ." The gross litany went on and on. "What's the matter, gonna cry? C'mon and cry, crybaby Davie. C'mon and cry, cry, cry, cry."

All around him, David could see the other passengers laughing at his humiliation, enjoying this ghastly joke of a grown man reduced nearly to tears by the sewer mouth of a little girl in pigtail ribbons.

"You shit-face, rat-turd, ass-licking—"

All at once, the El train emerged from the

tunnel, climbing once more into the afternoon. Momentarily blinded by the intense daylight, Labraccio blinked. And when he opened his eyes again, the little girl was gone. He looked around him. The other passengers were once again wearing their dreary, weary workaday expressions, and each of them was encapsulated in his own private pocket of exhaustion. It was obvious to David that they had seen and heard nothing.

There was nothing to see or hear. There never had been.

The train roared to a stop at the next station. An hour ago, it had started to rain; now, the concrete platform had little puddles already forming in the cracks. As soon as the car doors opened, David Labraccio pushed his way out of the car and ran up the stairs, taking them two at a time, never stopping until he'd reached the upper platform, out of breath. His heart was numb with fear and his legs and hands were trembling. He could feel his pulses pounding as he took in long, hard gulps of the icy wet air. His thoughts went spinning, and he found himself unable to slow them down.

What the hell was happening? He knew that little girl somehow. Although he didn't remember her name, he recognized her face, not only from his near-death experience, but from sometime early in his own life. And that was what was so strange; if that were true, that she actually came from his own past, then she wouldn't be a little girl today, but a woman in her middle twenties. Who was she? What did she want from him? Why had she attacked him so viciously? Most important of all, why had he called her up from the deepest parts of his soul?

Suddenly, David Labraccio knew with crystal clarity that his hallucination was connected in some way, not only to his near-death experience, but to Nelson's and Hurley's as well. Something in the experiment was wrong; something was terribly wrong. And Nelson hadn't told them. He knew, but he hadn't told them.

Rachel mustn't go under. He had to stop the experiment, one way or another. The whole thing had to come to an end before something happened that was too terrible to contemplate.

And suddenly, he thought of something else, too. Out of his boyhood he remembered the little girl's name. Her name was Winnie. Winnie Hicks.

The ceiling in the Dog Lab was old and cracking in places, and the rain was coming in. Little drips oozed through some of the cracks, while a steady downpour rained through others. Steckle and Hurley had rounded up as many buckets as they could find, and were performing a kind of triage with them, deciding which of the leaks needed buckets the most.

Rachel Mannus had already attached the EKG electrodes to her torso, and Nelson now checked the syringes, to make sure they were properly filled. Apart from the thunder of the rain into the buckets, there was a heavy silence in the lab; the customary raucous joking and coarse student humor was missing. Nelson and Hurley were unusually subdued, each of them lost in haunting thoughts, each of them pursued by private demons.

In addition, Nelson was not comfortable about Rachel's going under, especially for so long a time. Once or twice, he opened his mouth to say something to her, to issue some warning, but he said nothing. He couldn't find the words, or he didn't dare to make the admission that something might be wrong with his precious experiment. Most likely a little of both.

Rachel was not unaware of Nelson's jitters, but she attributed them to the fresh wounds on his face. He'd been beaten up again, this time even worse than before. His lip was split and swollen, and he really looked terrible.

"How'd that happen?" she asked quietly.

"Playing hockey." Nelson shrugged. It wasn't exactly a lie. Only it was Billy Mahoney who'd been playing, and Nelson was only the puck. "Look, about last night . . ." he began awkwardly.

Rachel cut him off. "It's okay."

For the tenth time in the last minute, Steckle looked at his watch. Nine-forty P.M. "No show Labraccio," he commented. "You know, this really isn't like him."

"It's just his way of trying to stop me," said Rachel with a stubborn lift of her chin that masked her disappointment. She'd been counting on Labraccio; his was the face she wanted to see just before the nitrous oxide became effec-

159

tive. "It won't work. I'm ready."

"We can't," Steckle answered worriedly. "Not without Labraccio. I don't think it's at all a good idea to do this without David."

"We don't need Dave," Nelson said shortly.

Rachel looked hard at Nelson. His hands were trembling. "Can you do this?" she asked him quietly.

He raised his eyebrow at her, and the ghost of his former coolness was back in his face. "Do you trust me?"

"No . . . but let's do it anyway." Rachel slipped off her blouse. She was still wearing her bra, but the EKG electrodes were attached to her body around it. Without another word she lay back on the gurney, under the refrigerated blanket, and smiled up at their concerned faces.

"See you soon," she said, in the instant before the nitrous oxide mask went over her nose and mouth.

He shouldn't have been in such a hurry to get off that El train; he certainly shouldn't have left the station. Why hadn't he just taken his truck to begin with? Now Labraccio was lost, roaming around in a part of the city he didn't recognize, and it was getting late. He found himself running down streets that led to dead ends or alleys. At last, rummaging in his jeans pockets to make sure he had enough money on him, he hailed a cab to the med school. Every minute of the long drive, he went over and over the same tortured thoughts, always coming to the same tortured conclusions.

The instant that David had remembered Winnie Hicks's name, an important piece of the puzzle fell into place, and he could begin to make out the picture, although not all of it. Now Labraccio understood what had been eluding him all along, ever since these insane experiments had started. Why hadn't he seen it before? Nelson had been acting strangely ever since his near-death experience, and Hurley, too. The two of them were covering something up. He was certain of it. Something to do with what they'd encountered, something that Rachel Mannus would encounter tonight, unless he got there in time.

If only Rachel hadn't been so stubborn! He had to stop her before she went under. He had to bring her back before she, too, became the target for whatever it was that was waiting out there for them.

The cab stopped at Taft, and David raced around to the side of the building to Nelson's secret entrance. It was late, very late, almost 9:45. He ran swiftly across the marble floor of the rotunda, not caring whether anybody heard his footsteps, down the corridor, and into the Dog Lab.

Rachel was lying still and deathly pale on the gurney, and the monitors showed two flatlines.

"How long has she been under?" he asked, out of breath.

161

"One minute," said Steckle.

"We're bringing her back."

"No, we're not," Nelson said angrily.

"Click that blanket to warm," Labraccio ordered. "What's her body temp?"

"Eighty-six," said Joe.

Nelson scowled. "She hasn't been under very long."

"Just do it!" Labraccio yelled, and Nelson reluctantly changed the setting on the refrigerated blanket. He gave David a nasty little smile.

"Don't expect any hugs or kisses for this one. She really wanted to go."

There was no tunnel, and there was no light, but five-year-old Rachel Mannus didn't miss them. She was so glad just to see the happiness in Mommy's face, and to be at the party. She loved a party, even when it wasn't her birthday. There was a big American flag hanging on the wall, and Mommy had painted a sign. Rachel couldn't read yet, she was too young, but Mommy had read it to her. It said, "Welcome Home Daddy." There was music, and Rachel saw her aunts and uncles and her grandpa and grandma dancing, and a wonderful big chocolate cake with "Daddy" on it in pink icing.

And there was this tall, handsome, strange man whom little Rachel didn't remember ever seeing before, but she loved him right away, because his blue eyes looked like the Sweet Lord Jesus's in the picture in the upstairs hallway, and because he picked her up and kissed her, and because he was wearing such a wonderful uniform with shiny-bright buttons and colorful ribbons. She touched the silver badge on his collar; it looked like a big balloon, but the man said it was a parachute, and that it stood for the 101st Airborne, and he was proud to wear it.

This was "Daddy," and they told her that he used to live here in this house with Mommy, but that he had to go away right after Rachel was born, and that he'd been away for a long time in a place called Viet Nam fighting a war.

And now he was home, so that was why there was a party, and why little Rachel felt so happy. Her Daddy was home.

"We're waiting for her body temp to rise," Steckle said into his recorder. "Eighty-nine degrees. Aborting fourth experiment. Why, Dave?"

"Why don't you ask 'Dr. Death'?" growled Labraccio, and he and Nelson exchanged angry looks. Nelson's eyes were the first to drop.

"Ninety degrees," Randy announced.

"What's going on here, Nelson?" Labraccio pursued him, and Nelson was suddenly aware that David knew something. Maybe something had been chasing him, too.

"Nothing," he shrugged. "We're bringing Rachel back a little early, that's all."

"C'mon, you guys," Hurley put in. "Don't start. Not now. Let's think about Rachel."

"Joe's right," Steckle seconded. "Ninety-one

degrees. Let's be ready." The resuscitation was going smoothly; Rachel would be back with them in only a little more than a minute now.

She'd been playing quietly with her dollie while Mommy was ironing, but now little Rachel was bored. She wanted her daddy. He was upstairs, in the bathroom. Maybe he was shaving. Sometimes, when he shaved his face, he let Rachel watch. She loved to watch. She loved the smell of the bubbly white lather that squirted like whipped cream out of a can, and the clean slick path the safety razor made on Daddy's cheek. She loved the sweet scent of the aftershave, when Daddy rubbed his smooth face on hers. She was going to see Daddy.

Standing up, Rachel laid her dollie down carefully so her baby would go to sleep, then she picked up her little tambourine that Daddy gave her and started up the stairs. As she went past the kitchen, she could smell the hot scorchy smell of the starch under the iron's surface, and see her pretty dark-haired mother in her apron, bending over the board. Rachel banged on her little tambourine with one hand, loving the noise it made. The tambourine sounded like a tiny drum, and the little cymbals around the edges jingled happily.

Something wasn't right. Nelson Wright slammed the defibrillator paddles against Rachel's chest, and the two hundred joules of current running through the girl's body jolted her. But nothing happened. Flatline on the monitors.

"Nothing," muttered Nelson, sweating. "Take me up to three hundred."

"Three hundred? You're hot." Labraccio recharged the defib paddles.

"Clear!" Nelson administered another strong jolt of electricity. "Nope, not a thing. Defibs! Clear!" And another zap. "Shit!"

The stairs were very long and high. Little Rachel didn't remember them being so long and high. She could see clear to the top, to the picture of the Sweet Lord Jesus on the wall in the corridor, His face so loving and a little sad, His blue eyes watching you. Mommy said that Jesus watched over you always, so that nothing would hurt you ever. Her five-year-old legs were getting tired, but Rachel kept climbing. She wanted to see Daddy. Daddy was in the bathroom. She could see the bathroom from the top of the stairs, but the door was only partly open. She'd have to push it open the rest of the way.

Still nothing. Nothing. Not a goddamn thing. Not one vital sign. Flatline. Nelson worked grimly over Rachel, and the sound of the water leaking through the ceiling and into the buckets was as loud as the drum section of a marching band.

The heart monitor blipped. "Got her!" Nelson yelled in triumph.

"We don't have her!" said David Labraccio

grimly. Behind him, the monitors showed flatlines.

Rachel could see Daddy now, through the partly-opened door. His back was turned to her, but he wasn't shaving. She put one small hand up and pushed at the door.

"No!" Mommy came up suddenly behind Rachel, grabbing her, pulling her away from the door, hurting her. The tambourine spun out of her other hand and landed on the steps. Why was Mommy hurting her? Frightened and confused, Rachel started to cry.

Daddy ran out of the bathroom, pushing Rachel and Mommy aside. Before anybody could stop him, he ran down the stairs, kicking the tambourine, which rolled all the way down to the bottom. Daddy ran out of the house, and Mommy ran after him. Mommy was crying, too, just like Rachel. Why was her mommy crying?

"That's okay, Nelson. That's fine." Randy Steckle was babbling a little, out of sheer nervousness. "We'll get her."

"Step me up to three-sixty!" ordered Nelson. "Clear!" He laid the paddles against Rachel's chest and she bucked upward. The heart monitor uttered a small peep, and the flatline wavered just a little. It was finally starting to happen.

Suddenly, the lights flickered, and a loud explosion of sparks came from the generator box and the socket outlet into which the defibrillator paddles were plugged. There was a sharp burning smell, and the generator went dead.

"What the hell's going on!" yelled Nelson. "I had her!" He looked frantically at the monitors. Flatline again.

"A short or a fuse, maybe a circuit," answered Labraccio, checking the box. He could see the problem immediately. Water leaking from the ceiling had made its way onto the panel and shorted it out.

"The backup battery!" Steckle remembered with relief. "Joe, you did charge it up, right?"

"Shit!" Hurley gasped. With all his problems on his mind, he'd totally forgotten. The battery was dead; they had no backup generator for the paddles.

Moving quickly, Labraccio pulled the plug of the defib paddles out of the wet socket, raced across the room to a dry socket, and plugged them in again. He rubbed them together. No juice, nothing. In the sudden surge of current when the box exploded, they'd burned out. Now they had no paddles. What the hell were they going to do without paddles?

She was afraid. Why was Mommy crying? Tears rolled out of Rachel's eyes and down her cheeks as she followed her mother down the stairs. But she had to go very slowly, one step at a time, and keep hanging on to the banisters, because her chubby legs were so short. When she got to the bottom of the stairs, the front door to the house was open. Rachel could see Mommy running down the street toward their car, still in her apron, and still crying. Scared, Rachel followed her.

"Starting CPR!" shouted Nelson desperately. "Steckle, bag her!"

Randy put the oxygen mask over Rachel's face, pumping the bag to regulate the flow, while Nelson kept pressing down on her chest. The disaster with the defib paddles had made everyone a little crazy.

"One-one-thousand, two-one-thousand, three-one-thousand, four-one-thousand, breathe!"

"No pulse," said Steckle, checking the monitors. Labraccio leaned in to place his stethoscope against Rachel's silent heart. He heard nothing.

It sounded like a car backfiring. The sudden loud noise made Mommy scream out. Rachel cried harder. This was so scary; she felt so afraid and alone. She'd never been alone before. Mommy never left her alone, but now she wasn't paying attention to the little girl trying to catch up, stumbling and running on baby legs. Mommy was looking at Daddy's car instead, and she was screaming and screaming.

Labraccio's mind raced over the options they had left. Without the defib paddles they were close to helpless; Rachel Mannus wasn't responding to the CPR or the oxygen. He checked the monitors.

"Nothing! C'mon, c'mon, Nelson, this is not working. Joe, take over!"

Hurley stepped forward to pick up the CPR rhythm from Nelson, who stepped back with great reluctance, glaring at David. But he wasn't ready to contradict Labraccio yet. David had taken over and seemed to be in charge.

"She's been under for four minutes," Steckle announced, panic making him hoarse.

Nelson grabbed a bottle off the crash cart, and plunged a sterile syringe into it. "We're moving to bretylium," he announced, expressing air from the hypodermic.

"No!" gasped Steckle. Bretylium was a really heavy-duty drug, unpredictable. Nobody knew how a patient's body would react to a sudden jolt of it. "Don't do it! You'll fry her!"

"It's the only way," Nelson insisted. He grabbed Rachel's lifeless arm, his fingers probing to find the vein.

David Labraccio leaned over the gurney, searching for Nelson's eyes. He caught and held his gaze. "Nelson, please . . . don't," he begged softly.

For an instant the two friends faced each other, and hidden meanings passed unspoken between them. Then Nelson Wright placed the needle carefully back on the crash cart and stepped back from the gurney.

"You bring her back," he said to Labraccio.

Rachel saw the hole in the car windshield. It wasn't a large hole, but it was perfectly round.

Little cracks radiated out from it in all directions. And there was blood all over the windshield. So much blood, so red. Little Rachel stared at the blood as it trickled down the glass to the dashboard. Once again, she heard her mommy cry out and pull her away from the door. She saw her father brushing past her, running down the stairs. She heard that loud noise again and her mommy screaming. And all the little girl could think was, *this is my fault.*

With feverish hands, David Labraccio pulled the oxygen mask from Rachel's face. Holding her nostrils pinched shut, he placed his mouth against hers and breathed into it, forcing his breath down deep into her lungs. Again he exhaled. Again. Again.

The ceiling cracks had grown wider under the pounding impact of the rain, and water was pouring in torrents into every overflowing bucket. The din was earsplitting. The faint sound of Labraccio's exhalations was completely masked by the rushing noise of the leaks. Three medical students stood as frozen as stone statues, hopelessly watching David Labraccio give Rachel Mannus mouth-to-mouth resuscitation.

Suddenly—"I hear something," Steckle whispered. "Shhhh. Listen."

Nelson and Hurley turned to look at the monitors. The flatlines were beginning to waver and peak. Now the little electronic blip was louder, stronger, more regular.

"O-2, O-2," yelled Labraccio happily, and

Hurley slapped the oxygen mask back on Rachel. They all stood watching the mask cloud a little with her breath, the bag move in and out like a bellows. What a wonderful, magical, beautiful sight! They were dizzy with relief.

"She's back," said David, grinning in satisfaction. Nelson Wright uttered a strangled sob.

— CHAPTER 10 —

Only an hour had passed since Rachel Mannus had returned, but to the others it seemed like an eternity. The interminable stress of bringing her back had drained the strength out of everybody; neck and shoulder muscles, released from tension, were screaming for mercy.

Labraccio was ready for some answers from Nelson, but he forced himself to be patient and say nothing until Rachel was strong enough to go into the women's lavatory to wash up. At last she did, and the other four hung around the rotunda, under the painted murals, talking quietly while they waited for her to come out.

"I still don't understand why you stopped us," said Randy Steckle.

Labraccio took a deep breath. This was the opening he'd been waiting for. "Listen to me," he said in a low voice. "There was this girl . . . Winnie Hicks. I went to elementary school with her. We . . . we used to make fun of her. Stupid kid stuff; we'd call her names to make her cry. Well, when I was on the train today, I heard someone calling me names. Really vicious, evil names. I turned around, and I swear to God she was standing there, right in front of me. And she was still only ten years old."

Nelson Wright flinched a little, but he said nothing. Joe Hurley's face was a study in anxious attention. Only Randall Steckle, who hadn't volunteered for the death trip, was able to scoff. "That's some hallucination. Maybe you fell asleep, and those thoughts and that kid were somehow triggered by submerged guilt."

"No, no." Labraccio shook his head. "I was not asleep."

Hurley took a step forward, and cleared his throat, feeling awkward but resolved to get this matter out into the open. "Guys, I've seen some strange things from my past, too." He laughed uncomfortably. "I thought it was brain damage."

Steckle's eyes lit up. "I gotta get this on tape," he said eagerly, fumbling with the Sony.

"Shut that thing off, Steckle," frowned Joe. "This is personal." Reluctantly, Randy pressed the stop button on the mini-recorder.

"Go ahead, Joe, go ahead," David Labraccio

174

encouraged. He glanced at Nelson, but Nelson kept himself apart, remaining silent and apparently detached. Even so, he was listening with both ears.

Hurley looked embarrassed; two spots of red burned high on his cheekbones, and he didn't look any of the others in the eye. "I've . . . uh . . . been haunted by these images of women that I videotaped without them knowing it. They're . . . uh . . . all members of the 'Joe Hurley Video Library.' " He stopped, unwilling or unable to say more.

Labraccio nodded, and looked significantly at Nelson Wright, taking in the fresh injuries on Nelson's face, his swollen nose and split lip. "What about you, Nelson?" he asked softly. "Who's come looking for you?"

Nelson shrugged and took a long drag on his cigarette. "It's no big deal. His name's Billy Mahoney. He's an eight-year-old kid we used to pick on in school."

"No big deal, huh?" Labraccio's voice was deceptively quiet. "Then why don't you tell us what happened to your face?"

Nelson smiled, and it was a terrible smile to see. "Sometimes the little fella gets carried away."

There was an instant's silence while the others absorbed this terrifying information. Then Randy Steckle gasped out, "Wait a minute! Wait! I can understand Dave nodding off on the train, and Pervert here having flashbacks, but are you actually saying that this kid physically touches you? He's *not* a hallucination. And it's *not* possible . . ."

"This whole lab's not possible." Nelson smiled painfully through his broken lip. "Or is it?"

Hurley backed off. "This is too weird," he mumbled.

Nelson's laugh was more like a short bark. "Weird? You want weird? We experienced death and somehow we brought our sins back with us, physically, and—" The smile vanished from his face. "And now they're pissed," he finished.

So there it was, out in the open at last. The heart of the mystery exposed and beating. They were being paid back for their arrogance in daring to go where they weren't wanted, in grabbing for knowledge that was not theirs to take. In the name of science they'd committed the sin of hubris against the unknown, and they now had to pay the consequences.

For their transgressions they were haunted, haunted somehow by past sins that had mysteriously taken on substance, sins which had come back with them from the other side of death, in the same way that a space virus will hitch a ride on a shuttle. The concept might be unthinkable, but the wounds on Nelson Wright were very real.

"And when did you know about this?" asked David quietly.

Nelson hesitated. "I had my suspicions," he confessed, "after Joe went."

Unbelievable! Rage exploded in David La-braccio's brain. "Before *I* went?" he yelled ferociously. "Before *she* went? You didn't say a word!"

"That was wrong, Nelson," said Randy quietly.

"Jesus Christ, I thought we were doctors . . . scientists!" Nelson yelled back.

"You call yourself a scientist?" Randall Steckle's voice quivered in indignation. "It was reckless, immoral and unethical for you to withhold findings from us!"

"Listen to me," said Nelson Wright quietly. "Rachel Mannus may hold the answers to life and death. She was under for five minutes! If she walks out of the ladies' room with those answers, the world will worship her." He pointed his cigarette straight at David Labraccio. "Like *you* do," he whispered with malice.

Furious, Labraccio turned around and stalked off in the direction of the women's bathroom, but he hurled his final words over his shoulder.

"You should have told us, Nelson."

"You wouldn't have done it!" Nelson called back. Scowling, he turned his back on Hurley and Steckle and, without another word, left the Taft building.

Randy and Joe exchanged horrified glances.

"We're fucked!" whispered Hurley.

Moving stiffly, Rachel made her way across and under the painters' plastic dropcloths to get to the sink. She turned both taps on, and waited for the water to gush out. But, when it came, it was only a trickle of rusty liquid from the ancient pipes. She watched in horror as it oozed slowly into the sink bowl. It looked like blood.

Nothing had been what she'd expected, nothing. All those first-person narratives she'd collected in her notebooks, all those accounts she'd read in her books on thanatology—none of them had anything in common with her own near-death experience. She'd seen no light, no tunnel, no garden. And as for the welcoming faces and outstretched arms of loved ones who'd gone before—Rachel shuddered, remembering.

It had been a nightmare, a nightmare of horror and blood, a total reliving of the day her father had taken his own life in the front seat of the family Chevy by putting a bullet through his brain with his service revolver. A total reliving of the worst day of her life. That wasn't how it was supposed to be. In all the accounts Rachel had heard and read, that wasn't the way it was supposed to be. It should have been beautiful, it should have taught her something, given her answers. Instead, she was left with more questions than ever, and this heavy weight of depression, guilt and . . . dread.

"Rachel, are you all right?" She recognized Labraccio's voice, but she didn't want to see or talk to any of them now, even Dave.

"I'm okay," she called out, in a voice that said go away. She turned back to the sink; the water was running clear now and Rachel scooped up a handful and splashed it on her face.

Behind her, the plastic dropcloths stirred. Rachel had the sudden impression that she wasn't alone.

"I said I was fine," she called out, irritated. She hated all the fuss the boys were making over her. There was no answer, yet she felt rather than saw somebody drawing nearer.

"You guys gonna watch me?" Who the hell was it? Labraccio? Hurley the molester? She was getting really angry now. Rachel wiped the water out of her eyes and looked up into the mirror over the sink. It was cracked all the way across, and now it reflected only a distorted image of her face and the bathroom behind her. Was anybody there?

She strained to see in the mirror, but was afraid to turn around. She couldn't look. She only knew that a dim shape, vaguely outlined in the broken glass, was standing behind her. And suddenly, an icy fist clenched at Rachel's heart. She knew who it was.

It was her father. And she knew he was very angry with her.

Nelson worked with frenzied concentration until the bolt was securely fastened to the door. When he was finished, the long black police bolt made of solid steel looked obscene against the pristine purity of the white woodwork, but that didn't matter anymore. It would do the job. Nothing could break through that, not even a tank. Not even Billy Mahoney.

He was sweating now in a mixture of exertion

and fear; his muscles trembled. The old Nelson Wright would have thrown off that wet and smelly shirt and showered for a long time, then put on fresh clothing. The old Nelson Wright was no more. No longer did he think about his personal cleanliness or the unsullied, antiseptic nature of his surroundings. He thought only about Billy Mahoney.

Making sure his back door was double-locked and all the windows were closed and locked, Nelson sat down cross-legged on the floor of his living room. In his hands, the palms of which were wet with fear, was the heavy screwdriver he'd used to fasten the bolt to his front door. Now all he had to do was wait, wait for Billy Mahoney.

Tonight he wouldn't sleep. This time he'd be ready for him. This time he wouldn't be caught off his guard. Nelson laughed out loud, crazily, defiantly, a weird echoing sound in the cavernous room.

"C'mon, Billy. C'mon. Give me your best shot." He tapped the handle of the screwdriver on the floor in a monotonous rhythm. "C'mon, I dare ya! I fuckin' dare ya!"

At last she fell asleep for a few hours, but it wasn't a deep restful sleep. Instead, Rachel Mannus skimmed just under the surface of sleep, dreaming fitfully, never sure whether she was asleep or awake. At last a small sound woke her, and she sat up in bed to see David Labraccio collecting a pillow and a couple of blankets from her closet, so that he could bed down on the couch in her living room. It was still dark out. Although Rachel had no idea what time it was, she knew that she couldn't have slept for very long.

"How are you?" he asked her softly.

Rachel didn't bother to reply. Something else was on her mind. She needed some answers to the questions that were torturing her. "Things from our past . . . they want revenge?" she asked him simply.

David looked at her with pity in his eyes. So Rachel was now haunted, too, just like the rest of them. Guilt from her past had hitched a ride back into life.

"I don't know," he said directly. "I'm not sure exactly how it works yet. But if you . . . see anything . . . I want you to talk to me about it, all right?"

Rachel nodded without speaking.

"Whatever you see, tell the doctor, okay?" Labraccio smiled at her, hoping that she understood he'd be supportive, no matter what.

Nodding again, Rachel laid her head back on her pillow. She was very tired. But she couldn't let it go, she had to know whatever it was that David Labraccio knew.

"Is it . . . people whom we've hurt or wronged in some way?" she whispered.

"Did something happen tonight?" countered David quickly. "Is there something you want to talk to me about?"

"No."

He hesitated, wanting to say more, hoping to get her to open up to him. Rachel obviously needed to talk. Whatever had happened to her when she was under, it had been terrifying. But she turned her face away, and seeing the pain in her beautiful eyes hurt him.

"Okay, just try to get some rest," he said at last. "I'll be right outside in the living room if you need me." He stopped at Rachel's desk, looking at some of the titles of her library of thanatology. *The Dying Patient. The Philosophy of Death and Dying. Beyond and Back.* There were others as well, all on the same topic, along with a stack of notebooks in Rachel's handwriting.

"Is it okay if I read some of these?" he asked. Rachel nodded, and Labraccio scooped up a handful of the books together with some of Rachel's notebooks, and carried them out to the living room.

Hurley and Steckle were waiting anxiously for him.

"How's she doing?" asked Randy as Labraccio came into the room.

David shook his head. "I don't know. I think she's hiding something."

"Like what?" Steckle persisted. "Is there any heebie-jeebie stuff going on in there?"

His words and the assumption behind them— that Rachel had shared her experience with him when in fact she hadn't—made Labraccio resentful. "How the hell am I supposed to know?" he burst out furiously.

Steckle backed off, his hands held up, palms

out, in the universal gesture of pacification. "Look, it's just really important that we keep each other informed, okay? You going to be all right here?"

Labraccio nodded wordlessly.

"Then we'll take off. C'mon, Joe."

David locked the door behind them and settled down on the couch, under the blankets, to read. In the bedroom, Rachel Mannus closed her eyes and wished for oblivion.

As hard as he tried, he couldn't stay awake. Nelson's head kept nodding forward, and he'd pull it back up with a jerk that made his neck ache, but eventually sleep simply overcame him, and the heavy screwdriver fell from his fingers.

He dreamed.

At first the dream was beautiful, the same dream he'd had when he was flatlined. He was Back There, running with his friends across that meadow, again, and they were playing that hide-and-seek game. They were after somebody, and they were running toward those trees in the distance. Nelson was leading the way, and Champ was barking happily and getting under everybody's feet, and the sun was very hot, and it was a beautiful day.

"Ollie ollie oxen-free!"

"Come out, come out, wherever you are!"

But "It" didn't want to come out. "It" was afraid to come out.

They were inside the little copse of trees now, stumbling over gnarled roots, and not finding what they were looking for. Champ found a tree, though, and stood on his hind legs with his paws on the trunk of a tall oak, barking with excitement up into the branches. He'd treed something; a small animal, maybe.

"Champ?" called Nelson. "What have you got there, boy?"

They looked up, all the way up into the crown of the tree. A little boy in a red, hooded sweatshirt was huddled on a high limb, pressed tightly against the trunk, watching them with fear in his pinched little face.

"It's Billy Baloney!"

"Come down, Billy!"

"C'mon down, we won't hurt you!"

But the boy clung more tightly. He knew better than to trust them. He wouldn't come down. Champ was barking and barking, and Nelson looked around on the ground for a rock. The right rock. His hand closed around it. . . .

His hand was empty. Nelson woke up from his dream with a start, to find himself sitting on the floor of his living room. Where was the screwdriver? He'd been holding on to a screwdriver. He looked up.

Billy Mahoney was standing in front of him, and in his small white hand was Nelson's heavy screwdriver. Before Nelson had a chance to think, or even to scream, the child raised it high in the air and brought the heavy handle crashing down on Nelson's head.

* * *

Rachel opened her eyes. The first rays of daylight were coming in through her bedroom window; it was very early in the morning. She must have finally fallen asleep, and had slept without dreaming for hours. She pushed back the covers, and was surprised to find herself completely dressed. Labraccio must have tucked her into bed that way last night. She stood up shakily. Every muscle in her body ached, and her chest hurt where the defibrillator paddles had slammed into her last night. Moving stiffly, Rachel washed her face and brushed her teeth, then pulled a shawl out of her closet and wrapped herself in it. She felt terrible, but there was something she had to do right away. Something vitally important.

Something moved in the bedroom; she caught a glimpse of it out of the corner of her eye. Gasping, she turned. Nothing; there was nobody there. But Rachel Mannus knew with certainty that somebody had been there, somebody was watching her, somebody wanted something from her.

Labraccio was still on the sofa, reading. He hadn't closed his eyes all night. When Rachel came into the room, he put her notebook down and asked, "How ya doing?"

"I'm late, I'll see you later," was all Rachel said. She headed for the door.

David pushed the blankets off himself and struggled off the couch. "Where are you going? Wait a minute—"

185

"I'm late." She didn't stop, didn't even look around. "I have to talk to her. I have to stop her." She sounded panicky.

"Talk to who? Wait—"

But Rachel was already out the door and running down the stairs. Labraccio started after her, then realized he wasn't wearing his boots. By the time he'd gotten into them and snatched up his leather jacket, Rachel was already out the apartment building door and running toward the bus stop on the corner. And by the time Labraccio hit the street, the bus had pulled up and she'd boarded it.

"Rachel! Wait! Rachel!"

But all he got for his trouble was a faceful of diesel fumes. "Shit!"

As soon as she reached the hospital, Rachel ran quickly along the corridor, down toward the ward.

"Morning, Rachel," said the head nurse, her eyebrows cocked in surprise. She'd never seen Rachel Mannus like this, her hair wild and uncombed, her shawl trailing after her like the White Queen in *Through the Looking Glass*.

"Morning." Hastily, Rachel threw the word over her shoulder. She ran into the ward, passing bed after bed, until she got to Mrs. Ashby's bed. Her terminal cancer patient. Her friend.

The bed was empty, and already made up with clean sheets and blankets. Two empty pillows sat, starched, white, and waiting, waiting for the next patient. A living patient.

Rachel stood frozen, staring at the empty

significance of the hospital bed. A moan of horror escaped her. "No! *No!* Nononono. . . ."

Edna came to stand beside her, placing one sympathetic hand on Rachel's shoulder. She could see that the girl was distraught.

"I wanted to tell her that her voices were wrong," Rachel wept. "There's nothing beautiful out there. It's terrible!" She sounded heart-broken.

"Rachel, you got to get used to losing them. It's part of our work," the nurse said gently.

"But I was wrong! I was *wrong!*" Bitter tears scalded her face.

David Labraccio went back to his old neighborhood, to Clairemont's S. B. Butler Elementary School. He parked the truck a block away from the schoolyard, not exactly certain of what he was doing here. But the day was so beautiful, more like May than early November, it would be good to walk around the old familiar streets for a while. Yet his footsteps carried him directly to the schoolyard.

The concrete schoolyard, with its old swings and rusting monkey bars, was filled with children playing. Labraccio heard before he saw it the slap of the jump ropes in the Double Dutch cadence, heard the little girls clapping in rhythm, chanting the jump rope rhyme . . . *Old Mother Witch couldn't sew a stitch, picked up a penny and thought she was rich . . . Old Mother Witch . . .*

The children were dressed in bright summer

clothing, jeans and T-shirts, sneakers and socks, cotton dresses. It didn't occur to David how strange this was for November. It all seemed so natural, so right. Children ought to have sunny days, they should be laughing, happy, with none of the cares of the adult world. Labraccio watched them a little enviously.

But they weren't all happy. One little girl was crying. A little black girl, no more than ten years old, with ribbons on her pigtails and tears coursing down her cheeks. She was surrounded by other children, and they were taunting her, insulting her, calling her stupid and ugly, pushing her up against the fence so that her back was to it and she couldn't move, couldn't run away.

With a shock, David recognized Winnie Hicks. And with a greater shock, he recognized the leader of the vicious little circle. It was himself, himself as he was more than fifteen years ago.

It all came flooding back to him, the names he'd called Winnie Hicks, the childish insults aimed like arrows at her heart, his wicked delight in the power he had to make a little girl cry. He'd forgotten how cruel children could be, forgotten how he'd been one of the cruel ones. The memory was so shameful that David Labraccio staggered under the weight of it. He would have fallen if he hadn't clutched at the wire fence of the schoolyard.

As soon as his fingers touched the icy metal, Labraccio's eyes closed. When he opened them again, the summer day had vanished, leaving him in cold November. The sun no longer shone warm in the sky. The children were gone; the playground stood silent, the swings empty, the monkey bars deserted. A few discarded newspaper pages blew across the concrete, chased by the wind.

He was alone, alone with his memory and his shame, both of which had been haunting him. And David Labraccio knew what he had to do.

It was getting really cold. Joe Hurley hurried from class, eager to be home. He needed to be alone, he had to think. Something really weird was happening to him, and little as he was given to introspection Hurley needed some time to figure out what the hell it was.

He turned the corner, his face to the wind, head ducked, and almost bumped into the darkly beautiful girl who was standing near his apartment building.

"You look like you're enjoying the day," she purred at him.

"Yes." But he wasn't really interested, he wanted to get upstairs.

"Don't you remember me, Joe?" She walked along beside him, smiling up into his eyes.

"Yes, of course," he lied. He didn't remember ever seeing her before.

"Are you a model?" the brunette asked him provocatively. "You could be."

The words brought the faintest echo of remembrance, but they made him uneasy. "Look, I have to go," he told her.

"I'm not picking you *up*." She smiled. "I'm

picking you *out*. Mind if I buy you a drink?"

"No, thanks." They'd reached his building now, and he opened the door, eager to get away from her. Why the hell was she so damn persistent? Couldn't she tell he just wasn't interested?

"I'll call you this weekend. I've been looking for a study partner."

"Fine. I'm in the book," Joe said brusquely, pushing past her and into his house. He checked to make certain the door was locked behind him.

"Hey, gorgeous," said a woman's voice behind him.

Surprised, Joe turned. A redhead, petite and adorable, was grinning up at him.

"Hey, I know you, don't I?" Hurley asked her.

The redhead smiled more widely. "Would you like to?" Her voice was husky, inviting. "We don't have to do anything. We can just lie together, hold each other, in our underwear."

Joe Hurley started. He recognized her words, and now he recognized the words of the girl in the street, too. They were his. His old lines. They were running his old lines on him. Why? Who were they? What did they want from him? He turned away from the redhead, and ran down the hallway to his front door, looking back over his shoulder to make sure the girl wasn't following him. She wasn't.

Unlocking his door with trembling fingers, Joe dashed inside, locking it behind him. He was home. Safe. He went up the loft stairs to his second story.

The loft smelled of perfume, different perfumes. It smelled of women. Jesus Christ, it was filled with women! Beautiful young women, enchanting, sexy, alluring, welcoming, and all of them were focused on him, all of them were talking to him, but the words they were speaking were his own. He knew them; he'd used those words too many times.

"I'll call you, I promise."

"I'm tired of playing the field."

"We can stop whenever you want."

"It'll only make our relationship better."

"I've never felt like this before."

"Of course I respect you."

"I need you to show me that you love me."

Lies. All lies. He was surrounded by his lies, choking on the seductive perfume of his lies. The women formed a circle around him, pressing closer and closer to him, their eyes undressing him, their hands reaching out to him—

"You're not real!" yelled Joe, and they vanished.

But the smell of perfume remained behind, and Joe Hurley knew that scent. It was Anne's.

She was sitting quietly on the couch, and she was real.

"Anne! Is it you? Is it really you?" Joe knelt at her side, and there were tears of relief in his eyes.

"You sounded so upset on the phone," said his fiancée, "I was worried. I took the bus down."

Her voice was strained, distant, unlike Anne's warm voice, but Joe was too happy to hear the difference.

"What a great surprise!" He leaned forward to kiss her, but she turned her lips away and Joe's kiss landed on her cheek. "How long have you been here?"

"Long enough to see your tapes."

His tapes! Joe looked around in horror. The videotape cabinet stood open, and sex-tapes were piled around the TV. "Oh, God!" he groaned. This was what he dreaded most in the world, that Anne should find out.

"Anne, I love you—" he pleaded, but the girl stood up from the couch, picked up her handbag, and started down the steps. She was outwardly very calm, but her voice trembled.

"You know," she said with tears in her voice, "the worst part of this is that you're going to think I'm leaving because you slept with all those girls—"

"It was just stupid!" interrupted Hurley in desperation, following Anne down the stairs. "An adolescent game. Those girls meant nothing to me." She mustn't leave him. She was the only person he loved, could ever love. And she loved him, too. He couldn't lose her!

"I wish they had meant something to you," said Anne, turning at the front door. Her large blue eyes looked reproachfully at him. "'Cause if you were honest, if you had cared for any of them, I could have fought it, because I loved you. But to film those girls, without their knowing it, to have so little respect . . . Those women trusted you, Joe. Every one of them trusted you. What kind of marriage do you think we could have when you have no understanding of trust?"

She pulled the engagement ring off her finger and placed it in his nerveless hand.

"No, Anne! Please! It's not what you think!" he begged.

Anne raised her head to look straight into his eyes, and Joe quailed underneath the honesty of her steady gaze. "Oh, yes it is," she said softly, and the door closed behind her.

Joe Hurley had never heard anything in his life more final than the closing of that door. With a sob of anguish, he sunk his head into his hands. He'd lost her.

— CHAPTER 11 —

There must have been three or four hundred numbers under "Hicks" in the telephone directory. Labraccio had no idea there were so many people all named Hicks. What the hell; if he had to dial each and every one of them, he would. But he hit paydirt on his sixteenth try.

"Hello, is this Mrs. Earl Hicks? Listen, I know this is kind of a strange question, but, um, by any chance do you have a daughter, Winnie? About twenty-six years old? You do? Great! Well, my name is David Labraccio and I went to school with Winnie. S. B. Butler. That's right, yeah. Yep, my parents still live in Clairemont. Oh, they're fine, fine. Well, I wanted to get in touch with Winnie, and I was wondering . . . by any chance, do you have her address? Great!"

With the phone still tucked under his chin, Dave grabbed up a pencil. "Uh-huh, uh-huh, got it. Thank you very much, Mrs. Hicks. I really appreciate it. Good."

Grabbing up his leather jacket, Labraccio pocketed the precious scrap of paper with Winnie Hicks's . . . no, now she was Winnie Johnson . . . address, and raced to his apartment door. He flung it open, and found Nelson Wright coming up the stairs. Shit, this was the last person he wanted to see. He didn't have time for Nelson now.

But when Nelson came into the light of the landing, David gasped. Somebody had been beating him up again, and badly. His head was covered with bumps and bruises, and blood matted his hair. Who was after him?

"Jesus!" Labraccio breathed. "You want me to take a look at it?"

"No . . . I just . . . wanted to know how Rachel was doing," Nelson said painfully through swollen lips.

"Well, she didn't come out of that bathroom with the answers to life and death," shrugged David. "I gotta go."

"Where are you going?" asked Nelson.

"Bensonville."

It was obvious to Nelson that Labraccio was in a hurry and didn't have the time or the patience for him now. Yet he had to ask. "Could I go?" he said in a low tone.

"It's a two-hour drive!" Dave protested, and

brushed by him to start down the stairs.

"Look . . ." The words were dragged out of Nelson despite himself. "Look, I don't want to . . . be alone."

Labraccio stopped and looked up at his friend. He'd never seen Nelson like this before. Nelson was always so controlled, so immaculate, so in command of himself. Now he was a filthy mess, and what's more, he stank. Compulsively clean Nelson Wright, who used up enough hot water to do the laundry of a good-sized suburb, stank. He smelled of stale blood, sweat, and sleeplessness and of something else. Fear, rancid fear.

For the first time, Labraccio looked past the scars and wounds on Nelson's head to the scars and wounds in his soul. He saw that Nelson's psyche was in tatters; whoever or whatever had been beating him had hurt him more on the inside than on the outside.

And David saw something else, too. Nelson had been battered very close to the breaking point, might already in fact have inched past it. His eyes were fathomless pools of pain; his voice held the sound of agony. He looked . . . terminal.

"Yeah," David said gently. "C'mon along if you want to, buddy."

"Today we'll remove the left kidney, then dissect the lower intestines," said Dr. Zho coolly, as though she were giving driving directions. "I would like you to remove the ascending colon from the transverse colon. Proceed to the sigmoid colon and on to the appendix. Remove the appendix, taking note of the blood supply. Next, we will enter the urinary bladder. . . ."

Rachel Mannus looked down at her cadaver, which lay on the anatomy dissecting table shrouded in gauze, its head masked. The corpse's belly had already been opened, revealing the coiled mass of the intestines, exactly like one of those toy store anatomy models which come apart layer by layer until only bones are left. She picked the scalpel up in her right hand. She was wearing throwaway surgical gloves, and the instrument felt strange and unreal in her fingers.

"Are you okay?" Joe Hurley's concerned face came up close to Rachel's, and he peered at her worriedly.

Her lips trembled a little. "I'd be fine if everyone would just stop asking me if I'm all right," she retorted in a muffled voice.

Rebuffed, Joe went back to his own cadaver, which was next to Randy Steckle's.

"Are you crazy?" hissed Steckle.

"Yes." Joe sighed. He must be.

"Is she getting the heebie-jeebies?"

"I'm the one who's spooking," Hurley complained. He'd told his old friend that his fiancée had walked out on him, but he couldn't bring himself to say why.

"Getting us kicked out of med school is not going to get Anne back. Get to work!"

Rachel bent over the cadaver, trying to keep her mind on the anatomy assignment and away from the darker visions that kept intruding themselves into her thoughts. But her hand trembled and she drew it back to steady it before she'd start making mistakes.

Her movement disturbed the gauze wrapping on the cadaver's arm, pulling it back to reveal the dead flesh underneath. It was a man's arm, muscular and strong. On it was a tattoo done in blue ink, a winged parachute. The insignia of the 101st Airborne. Her father had had one exactly like it. Rachel gasped in horror, and dizziness threatened to engulf her.

And now a wind from nowhere blew through the anatomy lab, and the mummy-wrappings on the cadavers were stirred by that wind. Under Rachel Mannus's terrified gaze, the body on her table began to rise, and the arm with the military tattoo became alive again. The hand turned, its palm upward, and it reached out for her. The swathed gauze on the head fell back, revealing a man's face, its mouth open in a silent scream. Its eyes were blank in death, yet those dead eyes were staring at Rachel, and they knew her.

It was her father.

Shrieking, Rachel backed away, crashing into the table that held her instruments, and knocking it over with a clatter. Then she ran, ran as though all the demons in Hell were after her. Ran for her life.

"Mannus! Rachel Mannus!" Professor Zho called angrily as the girl dashed from the anatomy lab.

Hurley and Steckle ran to the door of the lab,

but the diminutive Asian doctor barred their way. "I'll handle this," she said with crisp authority. "Get back to work or suffer the consequences."

Joe thought it over in a split second. A friend was in trouble, deep trouble, and it was partly his fault. For the first time in a long time, he was thinking of somebody besides himself. "Fuck this!" he growled and started after Rachel.

Steckle swallowed nervously. He had horrid visions of Dr. Zho's promised consequences, of his lost medical career, of what he'd tell his parents before they had matching nervous breakdowns. But Randy had balls, and nobody was more surprised about that than Randall Steckle himself. "Ditto," he said, running past the astonished professor and following Joe.

They'd driven for close to two hours, Labraccio with his eyes rather grimly fixed to the road, Nelson nodding off into uneasy sleep beside him on the front seat. City gave way to suburbs, and suburbs to countryside. They drove through Bensonville—population 3,000—and into the country just beyond it, a deeply wooded rural area.

All the way out, David went over and over in his mind what he would say to Winnie Hicks, but he knew that, once he saw her, he would say whatever he had to. If only it would work! He'd tried to explain to Nelson what it was he was trying to do, but Nelson was mired too deeply in his own private hell to take Labraccio seriously.

What Dave proposed doing might be all right for Winnie Hicks, but it would never, never be enough for Billy Mahoney.

"This must be it," said Labraccio, pulling up about fifty yards away from an isolated house surrounded by a large piece of wooded land. It was a very pretty setting, idyllic even. The house, built circa 1930, boasted a fresh coat of paint on the outside, and a deep shaded front porch from which wind chimes tinkled gaily.

Nelson roused himself. "Looks like Winnie did well for herself," he remarked.

Labraccio put the truck into park. "She's probably not even going to remember who you are," Nelson said.

David shrugged; that thought had occurred to him, too. Still— "It's worth a shot," he answered. "You coming?"

Nelson shook his head and grinned painfully. "Nope."

Labraccio got out of the truck cab, and hesitated. He was genuinely worried about Nelson. The guy was just stretched too tight, as strung out as a bowstring. "Look," he said slowly, "if anything happens, if you need me or anything, beep the horn. All right?"

"Okay." Nelson waved him off.

David started up to the house, turning once to see if Nelson Wright was okay. He saw his friend slouched down into the front seat of the cab, his feet up on the dashboard. Nelson kept his eye on Labraccio, who had reached the front door and was now ringing the doorbell.

"Ring, ring. Ring, ring," said Nelson out loud to himself, amused. "Dave, you should have sent a letter."

Nobody came to the door. Labraccio waited a minute, rang again, then he called out, "Hello! Is anybody home?" Silence greeted him, and he turned to go. But before David got to the front steps, he heard the door opening behind him. Turning, he felt his breath catch in his throat.

Little Winnie Hicks, ten years old, was watching him from the front door.

No, he could breathe again. It wasn't Winnie after all, but a little girl who looked very much like her. And she wasn't ten, she couldn't be more than six or seven. She had to be Winnie's daughter, a small replica of her mother.

"Hi," he smiled. "Is your mother home?"

The child regarded him gravely, saying nothing, and behind her a woman's voice called out "Coming." And then she appeared in the doorway. Winnie Hicks.

She was a grown young woman, not pretty but handsome. She was dressed for the country, in jeans and a turtleneck, and she had a good, sturdy figure, bright eyes and a clear brown skin. Her hair, no longer in pigtails, was cut short and brushed smooth around her face.

When she saw David Labraccio standing on her porch, a look of suspicion crossed her pleasant face, and she shooed her young daughter safely into the house. Plainly, she didn't trust him, appearing on her doorstep with his long hair and his black leather jacket. "Yes? Can I help you?"

"Uh, yeah, I think you can," began Labraccio awkwardly. "You're Winnie Hicks, aren't you? From Clairemont?"

She regarded him from a distance and her expression didn't soften. "Yes," was all she said.

"I'm David Labraccio. We went to S. B. Butler together? First grade? Second grade?"

"Really?" Winnie was still guarded. Whatever this white boy wanted, he was getting at it very slowly indeed.

"Yeah," David smiled lamely. "I just drove up from the city. That's my truck there."

Winnie turned her head and looked at the battered old army surplus truck with its canvas top. Another white boy was sitting in the front seat, and he had a face that looked like somebody had used it as a punching bag. He waved.

"'Hi,'" said Nelson in a whisper through clenched teeth, mimicking Labraccio. "'I'm nice, he's nice. We're both fucking lunatics. Can I come in, please?'" He saw Labraccio following Winnie Hicks inside the house. "I've gotta hand it to you, Dave. You've got guts." Scrooching down in the front seat again, Nelson dozed off.

The house smelled strongly of fresh paint and turpentine. David could see that renovations were under way; beyond the doorway in the dining room a ladder had been set up, and rolls of wallpaper were stacked, waiting. Winnie led the way to the kitchen, which was large, airy and bright, and very clean. It had been decorated country style, with fresh herbs growing in pots, and copper pans hanging on a rack from the ceiling.

There was a long deacon's bench against the wall; Winnie Hicks's daughter was sitting on it, and Labraccio perched next to her, a little awkwardly. Winnie said nothing, just kept her eye on David, obviously waiting for him to get to the point and tell her just what he was doing here.

"So, what's your name?" David asked the child.

"Sherry," she whispered back shyly.

"That's a nice name." Labraccio smiled. "Do you have any sisters or brothers?"

"Oh, no!" Winnie exclaimed. "Please, she keeps me busy enough."

At that moment, a tall handsome black man came in from the dining room, wiping paint splatters from his fingers with a turpentined rag. When he saw Labraccio, he said hello politely, but his eyes were on Winnie, and there was a question mark in them.

"Hi," said David.

"Ben, this is David. Labraccio?" She flashed her husband an answering shrug with her eyes.

"Yeah," Labraccio nodded. "I went to school with Winnie."

"Oh? That's great. Would you like a beer?"

"No, no thanks. Normally I would, but—"

"He has a friend in the car," added Winnie. It

was obviously a difficult situation for her; she had no idea what Labraccio was doing here or why he had come. How could she explain it to her husband?

"I guess you came to reminisce about the glory days," said Ben with a smile. "Nice meetin' you." And Ben went back to his painting.

David and Winnie looked at each other uncomfortably, and David realized that he was imposing his awkwardness on her and his time here was short. He'd better say what he'd come to say.

A rising wind rustled the dry leaves on the ground and sent them swirling. It grew stronger, shaking the heavy pine branches, making the needles whisper. Nelson Wright dozed on, curled in the front seat like a child, but his dreams were nightmares, and he groaned in his sleep. A small animal went running past the truck, and the sudden noise brought him awake. He looked around, uncertain for a minute where he was, then he relaxed. It was okay. He was out here in the sticks, in Labraccio's truck. Labraccio must still be in the house.

The animal ran by again, over there in the trees. Nelson caught a glimpse of it as it scurried by, in the rearview mirror. He saw a flash of red. It wasn't an animal at all. It was a little boy in a red, hooded sweatshirt. It was Billy Mahoney. Nelson screamed out in fear.

* * *

As soon as they were in the greenhouse, Winnie Hicks seemed to unbend a little. Holding on to her daughter's hand, surrounded by her precious plants, her babies growing in their two-inch and four-inch pots, she appeared to be a different person altogether, more confident and secure. The large, heated greenhouse was an important part of Winnie's identity. It was what she did for a living, raise plants for market.

Impressed, Labraccio looked around the long glass studio, seeing row after row of potted greenery—herbs, flowers, foliage plants, all of them healthy and growing.

"Wow, this is great, this is really beautiful!" he enthused. "You've done well for yourself."

Winnie smiled modestly, but there was definitely a gleam of pride in her eye. "Well, it isn't medical school, but I could never do that stuff anyway. I'm sure it's very difficult."

"No, you could have done it," David told her sincerely.

She shook her head no. "I never liked school. Wasn't too good at it. I'm surprised you even remembered me."

Winnie's words were the introduction he needed; they freed David to speak. He drew in his breath; this was very hard for him, but he plunged ahead.

"I do remember you. . . . I also remember the way I treated you back then."

He could see the look of sudden surprise in Winnie Hicks's eyes, saw her stiffen and take a step backward.

"I . . . I wanted to say I'm sorry." Labraccio looked at the woman earnestly, wanting her to understand, to accept what he was telling her and, ultimately, to forgive him.

Embarrassed, caught off guard, Winnie uttered a short laugh. "What are you talking about? That was so long ago," she said distantly. "I don't even remember what you could have done. Please, let's not dredge up all that stuff."

Little Sherry looked up at her mother with puzzled eyes. She sensed that something was not right. Mommy was holding her hand too tightly.

"Sherry, go on into the house," Winnie said shortly. "Go on, go *on!*" Reluctantly, the child went.

He had to say it all. "However we made you feel about yourself back then, it was wrong. We were wrong."

An expression of pain crossed Winnie's face, but she squared her shoulders and looked David straight in the eye. "I have a family now," she told him with pride. "I haven't been that ugly little girl for some time."

Labraccio felt a pang of shame shoot through him like a spear. "You were never ugly," he said.

"We were just kids," said Winnie Hicks quietly. "I know how kids are. It didn't mean anything." But it was obvious to David that it did, that the hurt of the memory was as sharp as the day it happened, more than fifteen years ago.

* * *

207

Almost panting in his haste, he moved like lightning, scrambling to lock the doors of the truck cab, frantically rolling up the windows. He couldn't see Billy Mahoney anywhere, but Nelson knew he was out there. Just waiting for his chance.

"David! Help!" he yelled, his heart thundering in panic. But behind the locked windows his voice didn't carry to the house. David couldn't hear him.

Winnie's husband Ben appeared suddenly at the entrance to the greenhouse, Sherry peeping out from behind him.

"Winnie, honey? Is everything all right?"

She nodded. "Everything's okay, Ben. I'm fine."

With a suspicious glance at Labraccio, Ben took the little girl's hand and left. He could see that Winnie really wasn't fine; she looked unhappy and upset. But whatever was going on between his wife and this long-haired white boy, it was no business of his. He trusted Winnie. If Winnie said it was okay, he'd take her at her word.

Labraccio could see the tear forming in Winnie's eye, and it cut him to the heart. He bit his lip. "I'm sorry if I made you feel bad. I didn't want to hurt you again," he said in a whisper.

She could only nod her head; her emotions made it impossible for her to speak.

"I'll go," said David, and he turned away,

defeated and depressed. It hadn't worked. The whole trip had been for nothing. Winnie felt worse than ever now, and it was all his fault.

The windows and doors were tightly locked. There was no way Billy Mahoney could get in. Then Nelson heard a flapping sound behind him, and his chest froze. He turned in the seat. The canvas cover of Labraccio's truck had worked loose at the back corner where David had laced it shut, and was now flapping in the November wind. Billy Mahoney could get in that way, through the opening in the canvas. With a cry, Nelson literally threw himself over the front seat into the truck compartment, landing in the middle of Labraccio's sports equipment, sending balls and bats and racquets flying.

There was nobody in the back. Thank God. His fingers stiff and awkward with fear, Nelson pulled the canvas cover back into place and laced it tightly shut. A sound behind him made him turn.

In the front of the truck, just coming over the seat of the cab toward him, was Billy Mahoney. And in his hands was David Labraccio's mountain-climbing pickaxe, a wicked thing with two points sharp enough to bite into a rock face, sharp enough to slice through human flesh.

Nelson screamed in fright, but there was nobody to hear him. Suddenly, he remembered Labraccio's words. *If anything happens, if you need me, just honk.* The horn, he'd forgotten the horn. Billy Mahoney stood between him and the horn, but that didn't matter. He had to get to that horn.

Frantically, Nelson tried to get to his feet, reaching past the little boy in the red, hooded sweatshirt for the horn on the steering wheel. That was when Billy Mahoney raised the murderous pickaxe high above his head and attacked.

"David. Thank you."

Labraccio turned back. Winnie Hicks was looking at him, and in her face, he could read the truth at last. She had not forgotten. She had never forgotten. The pain went too deep, and had lasted too long. She had recognized him the moment she saw him on her front porch, recognized him and was afraid again. It didn't make a difference that many years had passed, that now she was a woman who was loved and purposeful and happy in her life. Underneath all that still lived the miserably unhappy ten-year-old Winnie Hicks who'd been a target for abuse.

"Are you sure?" whispered Labraccio.

She nodded, and he could actually see in his soul Winnie Johnson open her hand and let that little ten-year-old Winnie Hicks go, fall from her fingers and depart forever.

It was over, and both of them were free of the nightmare. What David Labraccio had done for himself, he'd also done for Winnie. They looked at each other for a long time, and a kind of love passed between them, a love composed of understanding and freedom.

"Thank you," said David Labraccio, and he went.

This was a struggle different from any that had gone before. This one was to the death; Nelson knew that. If Billy Mahoney was strong in his previous attacks, his strength now was tenfold, and terrible. And in his hand was no puny hockey stick or screwdriver butt, it was a murderous weapon and he wielded it murderously. Nelson fought for his life, desperately trying to wrestle the pickaxe from Billy Mahoney's little fingers, but Billy wouldn't let it go. And Billy Mahoney was much, much stronger than Nelson Wright.

Something else was different, too, Nelson realized. The other attacks had been silent, voiceless. But now Billy Mahoney was laughing. His laughter was evil, not a child's laughter at all, but sharp as a razor, cutting into Nelson's brain, making him fight with greater desperation. He had to stop that laughter!

Over and over the two of them rolled, and with every passing second, the pickaxe came closer to Nelson's head. The most terrifying thing was, Nelson realized suddenly, that Billy Mahoney was playing with him. With his superior strength, he could plunge that sharp point into Nelson's skull whenever he wanted to. He was only delaying the moment in order to tease Nelson, to torture him by prolonging the agony.

Even with that chilling realization, Nelson

went on fighting to live. And to stop that fiendish laughter. But now the pickaxe was close enough for Nelson to smell the oil on it, and his struggles were getting weaker. . . .

Labraccio felt cleansed and happy as he left Winnie's house. He'd done the right thing; he knew it. Something told him that this would be the right thing for Hurley and Nelson, too. Make a clean breast. Expiate. Apologize. Atone. If he could do it, they could, too. As for Rachel, well, he didn't know what demon was haunting her, but David felt in his heart that the lesson he learned might serve her as well.

The wind had risen while he was inside the house; it was starting to get dark. Shivering a little, Labraccio drew the zipper up on his jacket, and turned the collar against his face for warmth. He began walking toward the truck.

Strange. Nelson wasn't sitting in the cab. And the truck was rocking on its tires, as though something was going on in the back of it. Labraccio began to run, calling out for Nelson. But there was no answer.

The cab doors were locked, and the windows of the truck were locked from the inside. David could hear angry sounds from the back, but he couldn't see through the canvas. What the hell was happening? Using his elbow, he smashed through the glass of one of the windows, reached in for the handle and pulled the door open. From the back of the truck came a thrashing noise and a muffled scream. Labraccio

FLATLINERS

scrambled inside and threw himself over the seat of the cab.

And then he saw . . . oh, God! . . . he saw . . . a battle to the death. Nelson Wright was fighting desperately for his life. He was being tossed around the back of the truck like a rag doll, by someone much stronger than himself.

But there was nobody else there! Nelson Wright was battling with an unseen enemy. He was clinging tightly to the pickaxe with both hands, trying, trying to plunge it into his own skull. Nelson was alone, but he was fighting as though all the devils of hell were his antagonists. He was fighting . . . himself.

In that split second of frozen horror, David realized that Nelson had been fighting himself all along. His dementia alone had caused those terrible wounds on his head and body. Nelson alone, and the ghost from his past.

"Nelson! Nelson!" Labraccio cried. "Stop!" He tried to prize the pickaxe out of Nelson's grip, but Nelson's strength was formidable, and he clung to it hard, all the while trying to kill himself with it, to bury it in his own skull.

"*Nelson!*" yelled David, grabbing the axe with both his hands.

Consciousness returned. Nelson looked up and saw Labraccio's face hanging over him. "Where's . . . where's . . . Billy Mahoney?" he panted.

"There's no one here but the two of us!" David shouted. "Let go, Nelson. Let go!"

As reality filtered in, the maniacal light in

213

Nelson Wright's eyes slowly faded. He understood that there was no Billy Mahoney; all along there had been no Billy Mahoney. These terrible wounds he bore on his face and body were self-inflicted. For the first time, Nelson realized the depth of the madness to which he'd descended, and the depth of the horror that was buried so deeply inside his soul.

"Oh, God!" he moaned, and he clung to Labraccio, weeping and shaking.

—— CHAPTER 12 ——

Nelson said hardly a word during the two-hour drive back to the city. He was badly shaken and dazed; to David he looked as though he was close to a state of shock. Labraccio hauled his old army surplus blanket out of the back of the truck, wrapping it snugly around Nelson's thin and shivering body, and fashioned a makeshift bandage for his bleeding face. As they reached the outskirts of the city, however, Nelson roused himself a little, and tried to pull himself together.

It was then that Labraccio told him about Winnie Hicks, about what had happened between them, and how it was finally resolved. Nelson listened, shaking his head in amazement. God bless David Labraccio. To him everything was so easy, so goddamn cut and dried. Just be rational, say you're sorry, all will be forgiven, and the worst shit would turn into strawberries and cream. Yeah, right.

Rationality, what a concept! It was enough to make the cat laugh. Or puke.

Knowing that he wasn't going to be able to leave Nelson alone tonight, Labraccio drove back to his own apartment building, intending to tuck Nelson in for the night. But when he pulled up, an outraged Hurley and Steckle came charging off the front steps where they'd been waiting. Labraccio could see Rachel huddling in the shadows of his front door, her coat collar pulled up around her face. She was very pale, and her eyes were burning and tortured.

"Where the hell have you guys been?" Joe demanded hotly as Nelson and David climbed down from the cab. "She freaked in class. We've been with her all day."

"How are you?" Labraccio asked Rachel, concerned.

"Fine. Just fine for someone who keeps running into her father who's been dead for twenty years!" Rachel uttered a short contemptuous laugh, a bark of despair. " 'Death is beautiful,' " she quoted sarcastically. "What a bunch of crap! How ya doin', Nelson? You okay? 'Cause I'd like to thank you. Thanks for the nightmare!"

Nelson glared furiously at Rachel, then around at all of them. "You were all so eager to

216

jump on my coattails," he sneered. "Welcome aboard."

"You withheld data! That's the same as lying!" yelled Rachel, as angry as he.

"I'm sorry you're all so upset," Nelson shot back in a mocking tone.

"You think you're the only one who risked anything or lost something?" An angry Joe Hurley leaped into the argument.

"I always thought there was something profoundly unnatural about the whole damn experiment," put in Randy Steckle.

Joe wheeled on his old friend at once, livid with rage. "Talk about somebody who hasn't risked a goddamn thing!" For a minute, the others thought he was going to punch Steckle out. Evidently Steckle thought so too, because he flinched and backed off a foot or two. "Screw yourself!" he yelled from a safe distance.

This was beginning to take on all the earmarks of a common brawl, each of them turning on the others, each determined to assign blame to the others. As the voice of reason, Labraccio tried to make peace. "C'mon, c'mon, this is not gonna help!" he pleaded. "We're in this together."

"No, we're not," stated Rachel flatly, and she turned and started to walk off.

"Isn't she strong! So independent," jeered Nelson at her retreating back.

She whirled to face him, and her eyes flashed with rage. "At least when I get into trouble, I don't drag everybody down with me."

217

Nelson's eyes narrowed in sarcastic malice. "Come on, what happened to you, huh?" He rounded on Joe. "You got caught with your videotapes down. Wow!" He turned to David. "And you swore at a little girl on a playground. And you," he shot at Rachel, "you're having bad dreams about Daddy. Well, I'm real-ly sorr-ry."

Stung by his mockery, Rachel stalked back and came up close to Nelson. "You don't know anything about me, Nelson. You never have."

"No, but Dave understands you, doesn't he?" he cooed at her viciously. "Hey, they're your sins. Live with them. I do." Nelson grabbed at her coat, pulling her closer still, until her angry beautiful face nearly touched his angry battered one.

"You wanna see death?" he taunted her. "Take a good look. It is beautiful, isn't it?"

Rachel recoiled from the sight of his fresh wounds, but more from the flicker of madness in Nelson's green eyes. David Labraccio threw himself between her and Nelson, pushing him aside. "Leave her alone!" he commanded. "You already hurt yourself. What do you want? You want to hurt her, too?"

Rachel wheeled in disgust and marched off. Instantly, David took off after her, but turned back suddenly and said to Joe, "Help him find Billy Mahoney."

"Why me?" yelped Hurley. "I have to study."

"Damn it, Joe! Just don't leave him alone! Help him find Billy Mahoney!" And he ran off to catch up with Rachel.

Joe turned resignedly to Nelson. "Why do we have to find Billy Mahoney?"

Nelson shrugged. "Because 'Doctor' Dave thinks he's solved our karmic problems," he said lightly. "Atonement, gentlemen, atonement."

Rachel was walking so swiftly that Labraccio had to break into a run to catch up with her. "Wait a minute, wait a goddamn minute! Jeez, you're always running away. Why don't you talk to me?"

She stopped, hesitating. What David Labraccio was saying was true. She always did run away, not only from him but from everybody. She felt so confused, so frightened! If ever she needed a friend, somebody to talk to, that time was now. Her eyes met David's, and she saw such kindness, such intelligence and sensitivity in their expression that she could only nod her agreement. If she tried to say anything now, she'd cry, and above all she didn't want that.

He took her back with him to his apartment, to that huge beautiful poster over his bed, the one that held his most precious private dream of tall mountains, and they sat and they talked. And Rachel, struggling with her feelings, struggling not to break down and weep, told David what she thought she'd never tell anybody, the deepest and most painful secret of her life's core.

"My father shot himself when I was five," she said.

David thought this over a second. A parent's

suicide explained a great deal about Rachel Mannus—her retreat from people, her shyness, her preoccupation with death. "And you feel responsible?"

Her eyes filled, but she managed to go on in a strangled voice. "There was this door . . . in our hallway . . . and I wasn't supposed to go in . . . I guess . . . somehow . . ." She broke off and couldn't continue.

"Come on, Rachel," said Labraccio gently but firmly. "Kids always feel responsible. You couldn't have been to blame."

She nodded; intellectually she knew his words were true. A five-year-old child can scarcely be the cause of a grown man's suicide. But feelings are not intellectual; emotions are never rational. She knew what she knew, and besides, her father was back, wasn't he? Haunting her, reaching out for her, wanting to pull her back with him, into the grave.

"David, you said it yourself!" she cried out in agony. "People we wronged want revenge!"

Labraccio came closer to her. He sat down next to her on the sofa, and took her hand. "Look, I don't know if this is going to help," he began, his eyes searching hers. "Going to see Winnie Hicks today . . . I don't know how to explain it . . . but, somehow, just asking for forgiveness . . ."

"Winnie Hicks is alive!"

Labraccio could feel her resistance. Like Nelson, Rachel didn't believe there could be any comparison between someone living you could encounter face-to-face and something that reached out for you from the other side of death. He grabbed her by the shoulders, forcing her to look at him, to listen to his words.

"Rachel, your father is in a good place. And he wants you to let him go!"

Oh, God, could David be right? Could that be true? If she could only believe it! She wanted so much to believe it! A sob was torn from her. David threw his arms around her, hugging her tightly, comforting her, while Rachel allowed herself to weep at last. She cried and cried, while he just held her and stroked her hair and soothed her like a parent does a child.

Then, suddenly, they were kissing. David's mouth was warm on hers, sweet and loving, then passionate and insistent, as Rachel kissed him back. She needed him; she realized it and it didn't make her unhappy, this need. Because he needed her, too. As he pulled her more deeply into his arms, she went willingly, eagerly, understanding that the living must call to the living, and that death must be put aside in the face of it.

"Here," said Nelson and Joe braked his old black Mustang to a stop.

"Where the hell are we?" Hurley wanted to know. Nelson had taken them to the ass-end of nowhere, just a bunch of houses and yards, about ten or twelve miles from the center of the city.

"Don't you think we ought to get you to a hospital and have your face looked at?" Steckle pressed. It was so dark out they couldn't see a damn thing, and he was nervous about dragging around a strung-out Nelson Wright who'd so obviously flipped.

Suddenly, Nelson's hand snaked out and grabbed the car keys out of the ignition. Before Hurley could protest, he pushed open the door and was off and running.

Randy and Joe scrambled after him, shouting, but Nelson didn't look back. He moved quickly and surely through his old neighborhood, cutting across the yards and the back alleys. All the other two could do was trail after him as best they could.

"Come on!" Nelson called out, laughing. "This is a short cut. . . . I'm surprised I remember all of this. . . ." He ducked through a jagged hole in a brick wall. "Holy shit! The neighborhood's really fallen apart!" He ran down an alley, turned around a corner, and disappeared from sight.

"Gimme the keys, Nelson!" Hurley yelled into thin air. Dogs were waking up in the yards and barking all around them, and he could see lights going in upstairs bedrooms. Soon the whole damn town would be after them, probably with shotguns. Nelson was really far-gone crazy, and Steckle was already running out of breath, panting, bitching and moaning about how the fuck were they gonna get back?

Suddenly, Nelson's head popped up over a fence, grinning. He seemed to be . . . a little kid again, as though he were regressing into his childhood. "Shhh, don't wake up Mr. Shapiro, he's mean."

He ran off again, with the other two following. It was like a kids' game of tag or follow-the-leader through the backyards of strangers. Clean laundry hung from clotheslines, flapping in the darkness like colorless shrouds. Randy and Joe pushed their way through sheets and blankets that threatened to entangle them; it was stone creepy.

"Step on a crack, break your mother's back," Nelson singsonged up ahead, just like a little kid, and that was even creepier. Steckle and Hurley exchanged puzzled glances, consternation in their faces.

"Ollie ollie oxen-free." Nelson came to a momentary stop at a low stone wall. "Last one over is a rotten egg. Come on, boys, salvation just ahead!" He vaulted over the wall and disappeared. After an instant, Hurley jumped over, and Randy followed, more slowly and with a lot more effort.

They landed on soft earth. There was no concrete under their feet, no houses around them. Straining their eyes, Steckle and Hurley could make out strange shapes in the landscape, large blocks of stone, and marble crosses. With sudden clarity they knew where they were.

"This is a graveyard," Steckle breathed. This was so weird! For the twentieth time, he wished that he was anywhere else but here.

"Where the fuck are you, Nelson?" yelled Joe. "This isn't funny!"

"It never was," Steckle whispered.

"I'm right here." Nelson's voice, now subdued and no longer childish, came from thirty yards away. They turned and peered. Nelson was kneeling on the ground near a large ivy-covered tombstone.

"This is where Billy lives. Wake up, you little shit! You've got company."

Slowly, their eyes adjusting to the darkness, Joe Hurley and Randall Steckle approached the stone. They realized somehow, without articulating it even to themselves, that they were caught up now in Nelson's own secret fantasy, and in this moment they were nothing more than witnesses to his destiny. Something terrible was being worked out in this place of death, and they were powerless to stop it.

Nelson looked up at his classmates, and his battered face wore a dreadful expression, half ecstasy, half despair. "You want to know how I knew where he was?" he whispered. "'Cause I put him here."

The headstone was so overgrown with ivy that leaves had obscured the inscription. Gently, almost lovingly, Nelson plucked at the leaves, smoothing them away from the carved words— "In Loving Memory of Billy Mahoney, Born 1965, Died 1973."

He felt the leaves under his fingers. He felt the leaves . . . the leaves . . .

Leaves fell from the branches as the running boys gathered around the tree where Champ was barking furiously. Nelson found the stone he wanted, round and large and hard, a good stone for throwing. He had a great pitching arm for a nine-year-old, and he was fussy. The others had picked up stones, too, and were jeering up into the branches.

"Billy Baloney!" "Yah, Billy!" "Come down, Billy Mahoney."

Up on a high tree limb, a little boy in a red, hooded sweatshirt clung to the trunk and looked down in terror. Of all the boys who were taunting him, he feared Nelson Wright the most. "Please, Nelson, don't!" he begged, tears streaming down his small, pinched face. "Don't do it! Don't!"

But Nelson had already cocked his hand back. As though it possessed a will of its own, the stone left Nelson's hand and flew high, high, up into the tree. Oh, how swiftly and accurately it flew! Just like a feathered arrow. It slammed into Billy Mahoney's temple. The boy tottered, his head snapped back, and he let go of the trunk.

Billy fell. He fell slowly, down, down through the branches, while Nelson looked on in horror. He broke branch after branch with his fall, yet still he kept falling. And, as he fell, Billy Mahoney screamed. He screamed and screamed, and never stopped screaming, while Nelson now screamed, too. And their mingled screams of fear were joined by a yelp of anguish as a heavy branch fell on Champ, breaking the dog's spine.

They were lying on the ground, the boy and

the dog. The boy lay very still, while the dog slobbered and twitched and howled in agony, a death howl. Nelson looked on in horror. Nelson Wright, nine years old . . . he had done this thing. He was a bright, shining, brilliant, happy, beloved, yellow-haired boy whose aim was true and whose hand was strong, who had picked up a stone in a wicked little child's teasing game that had gone too far and killed Billy Mahoney. He'd made Billy Mahoney dead, and Champ, too.

"I was taken away from my family when I was nine years old," Nelson finished. Bitter salty tears trickled one by one down his cheeks. "I was sent to Stoneham School for boys. I thought it was over."

"Nelson, it was an accident," said Joe in a hushed voice.

"Let's go home, okay?" whispered Randy gently.

But a strange look came over Nelson's face. His green eyes began to glitter through the tears. "Dave was right," he breathed. "I can still make amends." He stood up, turned, and broke into a run. "Joe, I gotta borrow your car!" he called over his shoulder.

"Wait! Nelson! Wait! Come back!" Hurley started after him, but it was already too late. Nelson had vanished.

The two of them stared at each other helplessly. Nelson had taken the car, and they were marooned here, in a night-struck and probably haunted graveyard in some nameless godforsaken place.

"Oh, my God!" whispered Steckle.

Something woke Rachel. Was it a sound? A movement? She wasn't sure, but she came awake with all her senses straining. Next to her in the big bed under the Himalayas poster, David Labraccio went on sleeping, his breathing deep and regular. There was comfort in his steady presence, in his muscular arm wrapped around her, and in the sweet lingering memory of their lovemaking. But Rachel wanted no comfort now.

She pushed David's arm off her and rose silently from the bed, putting David's old bathrobe on over her nakedness and pulling the belt tightly around her waist. Her feet moved silently across the bedroom floor toward David's bathroom; she felt a strong attraction coming from the other side of the bathroom door. Somewhere in the back of her consciousness Rachel heard a telephone ringing, but she paid no attention. The bathroom pulled her forward like a magnet pulls scraps of iron.

The bathroom door was closed, but she pushed it open and slowly walked in. The little room seemed much larger than Rachel remembered it, and different. Familiar, not familiar. She realized suddenly as if in a dream that it wasn't David's bathroom she was in at all, but the old bathroom in the house where they'd lived before Daddy died. She was afraid, terribly

227

afraid, but she kept going forward, knowing that something up ahead was waiting for her . . . waiting for her . . .

"Rachel!" There was a loud knocking on the bathroom door, and she heard David's voice calling her name. She turned, and the door opened. The vision faded, and she was standing in David Labraccio's bathroom again.

Labraccio had pulled on his jeans and was hurriedly buttoning his shirt.

"Nelson freaked out," he announced. "Joe and Steckle are stranded. I gotta go get them. Will you be all right alone here?"

"Yes," she nodded quietly.

"Sure?"

"Yes."

"Good." He turned to go, then turned back to her. Cupping Rachel's beautiful face in his hands, he kissed her briefly, but with love in his touch. He picked up his jacket, searched it for the truck keys, gave her a flashing smile of reassurance, and was out the door.

Rachel was alone. There was no way she could go back to sleep again. She felt a terrible sense of foreboding—something awful was going to happen, something violent, and there was no way she could stop it. Uneasiness kept her moving around Labraccio's apartment. She thought of turning on lights, but somehow she didn't. Somehow she found the scary darkness fitting. For a minute or two Rachel wandered in the dimness, making certain to stay clear of David's bathroom. She wanted to wash up, but she didn't dare. Something terrifying was in there; she was convinced of it.

Rachel walked through the living room, her fingers trailing along the walls, a shiver caught in her throat. When she reached the far end, she found herself looking up a long flight of stairs.

Stairs! There were no stairs in David Labraccio's apartment!

Oh, but she knew these stairs. Rachel recognized them right away. She was in her old home. There, on the wall at the head of the staircase, was the painting of Sweet Lord Jesus, and His blue eyes were gazing down at her in pity and sorrow. Here, on the step near the bottom, was her little tambourine, the one Daddy had kicked aside when . . . when . . .

He was waiting for her; she knew that as well as she knew anything in this life. She mustn't go up those stairs. A sudden scorched smell reached her nostrils, and Rachel looked over to see Mommy ironing in the kitchen; it was the hot starch she was smelling. Mommy was so pretty in her apron. But where was Daddy? She wanted to see her daddy.

One step at a time, with agonizing slowness, Rachel Mannus climbed the staircase. She could see the corridor leading to the bathroom, the room she wasn't supposed to enter while Daddy was in there. She moved forward as in a dream, her feet making no sound.

The bathroom door was partly ajar. Rachel reached out one hand slowly and pushed it open. He was in there, his back to her. He was wearing

229

his service pants and a khaki undershirt and his arms were bare, his shoulders strong and bony. Rachel came up wordlessly behind him, and looked over her daddy's shoulder. Now she was tall enough to see.

She saw a spoon, its bowl burned sooty black with matches, and in the spoon, the heroin was cooking. As Rachel watched in dreamlike helplessness, Daddy plunged a syringe into the spoon, filling it with the colorless liquid. A piece of rubber tubing was wrapped tightly around his upper arm, the ligature bringing out the vein just above the Airborne tattoo. She saw the needle poised over the arm, she watched as it sank in deep and the junk flooded hotly through her daddy's vein.

A small cry escaped Rachel's lips, and he heard it. He turned to look at her, and for the first time as a woman she saw what she could not see as a child.

Daddy was young, so terribly young, little more than a boy. He was her own age, twenty-five, and he was frightened. Her father was a drug addict, one of the thousands who'd been wounded in that terrible war, who'd become addicted to the morphine the hospitals had given to ease their pain. From the Opium Triangle they'd returned with their addictions, these veterans, and nobody understood, nobody was there for them. Daddy was afraid and alone, and sick. Heroin was so easy to find; a five-dollar bill got you a nickel bag on any street corner.

She turned away from the pitiful sight, and her heart broke in her breast because she'd been too young to understand, too young to help.

Daddy looked at Rachel. Sweat beaded his forehead, tears stung his eyes. She was his baby, his precious little girl, and he was helpless to explain to a five-year-old why her daddy was sick, and why his days and nights were such unendurable torment. But to Rachel the woman he was able to speak at last.

"Rachel, sweetheart. Rachel, I'm sorry."

His trembling arms came up, reached toward her. With a little cry of pity and understanding, Rachel threw herself into them, and they stood together tightly entwined. All the love and sympathy in her nature she poured out to this poor, addicted fragment that had been her father.

"Will you forgive me?" he begged.

That was what he'd wanted from her all along, why he'd followed Rachel back from death. He'd wanted her forgiveness; her absolution was the only thing that would set him free.

"Atonement," David had said. He was right. Rachel had granted her father his own atonement, and now they would both be at peace.

Labraccio pulled up in his truck. Hurley and Steckle dived into the front seat and they took off.

"What the hell happened?" David demanded.

"Billy Mahoney died seventeen years ago," explained Steckle. "And whether he actually is

231

or not, Nelson feels responsible."

"Jesus Christ! Have you any idea where he went?"

"He ran off mumbling something about making amends," Steckle said.

"He's out of his mind!" cried Hurley. "How can you make amends with somebody who's already dead?"

A dreadful possibility flashed into Labraccio's mind. "You don't think he'd try to flatline without us, do you?"

There was a moment's horrified silence, then Steckle breathed, "That would be suicide!"

Labraccio merely nodded, but he stepped hard on the gas pedal.

Rachel lay curled up on David's bed, enveloped in the most perfect feeling of peace she'd ever known. Her nightmare was over, and she was happy, happier than she'd ever been. Soon David would be back, and she could tell him what happened, tell him how right he was, and thank him.

The telephone rang, and she snatched the receiver up eagerly. "David?"

"No, it's Nelson."

"Nelson, where are you?" she asked, alarmed.

"Rachel, I wanted to say I was sorry. Please tell David I'm sorry for ever getting any of you involved in this—"

"You don't understand!" she cried eagerly, wanting to share her happiness with him and set his mind at ease. "None of that matters now!"

His laughter took her by surprise. He sounded confident, almost like the old Nelson, yet there was a note of something else. All the pretense was out of his voice, and he sounded resigned, almost peaceful.

"No, Rachel," he said gently. "Everything matters. Everything we do matters. That's why I'm going under again."

Going under! Alone? "No!" she gasped. "No, Nelson, wait! Listen! Please wait!" Oh, God, he didn't understand! Why couldn't she make him understand? She had to stop him.

"Goodbye, Rachel," he whispered. "I really am sorry." There was a terribly finality in the click, and the line went dead.

Nelson hung up the receiver, and stepped out of the phone booth. The streetlights on the university quad outlined the Taft Building with an eerie halo. There was no moon. He began to walk quickly, then to run. He knew the others would soon be looking for him. He didn't have much time.

CHAPTER 13

We've been paid back for our arrogance," was Steckle's opinion. The truck was racing through the night toward the Taft building and the Dog Lab.

"Save it, Randy," snarled Joe.

"It's a good thing I didn't flatline," Steckle went on morosely. "My 350-pound babysitter would be running after me, waving the half-eaten pastrami sandwich I stole from her."

Joe Hurley didn't answer. His thoughts were on his own predicament, and he was weighing Labraccio's solution to it, finding it hopeful yet daunting. To actually apologize to every girl he'd ever taped? To look each and every one of them up, admit his transgression, and beg for forgive-

235

ness? Would it work? Would Anne come back to him if he did it? God, if You get us out of this mess, I promise . . .

Labraccio said nothing, but grimly kept his eyes on the road and his foot on the gas. His heart was pounding with dread. Nobody had the insight into Nelson that he had; none of the others knew the depths to which he was capable of going in his *extremis*. He had to get there before it was too late!

Something else occurred to David, an insight into himself as well. He thought suddenly that perhaps the wrong he'd done Winnie Hicks all those years ago, and the secret guilt that had haunted him ever since, had somehow made him a better person. Perhaps that was why he went into medicine in the first place, wanting to be a healer. To make up for the wrong he'd done. And maybe, just maybe, that was why he did things like laying his career on the line for a woman who was bleeding to death—to expiate, just a little, the sin he'd committed against a fellow human being a long time ago. Wouldn't that be something if it were true?

He thought of Rachel, and the ice in his belly thawed a little. If anything good could be said to come out of this insane experiment of Nelson's, it was that David and Rachel had found each other. He remembered her sweet face on the pillow after they'd made love earlier, the way her dark auburn hair tumbled over the pillowcase. He wanted to stop and phone her, but he knew he couldn't afford to waste even a few precious seconds.

Labraccio didn't know that, even now, Rachel was racing through the streets on her way to the Dog Lab.

Nelson Wright pounded into the Dog Lab and raced to turn on the work light by the gurney. He threw off his coat and rolled up his sleeves. His eyes were wide, his brow was covered with sweat, and he could feel his breath rasping harshly in his chest. Never mind, it would all be over soon.

His hands searched feverishly among the bottles on the crash cart. He picked up the sodium pentothal, and put it down again. Not what he was looking for, not strong enough, not final enough. There, that was it! The potassium. That would do it, all right.

Nelson knew the others would be coming to find him, and for their sake, and the sake of the final experiment, he attached the EEG leads and the EKG electrodes to his body. As for himself, he had no need of them. Where he was going, he wasn't coming back. He switched the refrigerated blanket to its coldest setting, and inserted a sterile needle into the bottle of liquid potassium. Then, wrapping a rubber tube around his arm to bring out the vein, Nelson climbed under the blanket, and with a great effort, plunged the syringe all the way into his arm.

He lay back on the gurney, feeling the drug

beginning to take hold. Quick, before he fell unconscious, the nitrous oxide. Nelson groped for the mask, and found it, switched on the flow of the anesthetic gas.

"Okay, Billy Mahoney, come on!" he challenged, and placed the mask over his face. His eyes closed, and his breathing became shallower and shallower. . . .

And stopped. Nelson's heart stopped beating. Flatline.

He was hurtling backward in time, fighting for his life again, Billy Mahoney on top of him with the pickaxe, laughing in his face as he threatened to bash in Nelson's head. Billy Mahoney slamming him in the face with the screwdriver. Billy Mahoney with the hockey stick, breaking it across Nelson's back and shoulders, beating him, kicking and punching him viciously. Nelson sobbed in fear.

Now the sun was hot on the field, and the grass was springy under his sneakers as Nelson ran. But he didn't feel the softness of the grass, only the pounding of his heart and the rasping of his breath. And the fear, that awful rending fear.

It was him they were chasing now, all of them, and Billy Mahoney was in the lead, running after him, jeering. Champ was chasing Nelson, too, but in his happy excitement he kept running under Billy's feet, slowing him down. Nelson knew what would happen if they caught him, and it made him afraid. If he could only reach those trees! He was a good climber, and if he could hide up there, they might not find him.

Labraccio pulled up in front of the Taft building and the three of them hit the ground running, racing around to the side entrance. They sped across the rotunda to the long corridor that led to the labs, Hurley in the lead, Labraccio next, and Steckle puffing along behind.

As they raced into the Dog Lab, Labraccio hit the overhead lights, and ran to the gurney. Nelson was lying peacefully, his eyes closed. Two flatlines showed on the monitors. They had no idea how long he'd been dead.

"Body temp seventy-eight!" called Hurley. The monitors registered no heart or brain activity.

"Oh, God!" moaned Randy Steckle. Nelson looked so very dead lying there.

Labraccio switched the refrigerated blanket to its warm setting. Rummaging through the bottles on the crash cart, looking for antidotes, Steckle made a terrible discovery.

"Potassium! He used potassium!"

They exchanged horrified glances; potassium would make resuscitation infinitely more difficult, if not impossible.

"Calcium in!" announced Randy, while Hurley charged up the defibrillator paddles.

"Three hundred! Clear!" yelled David, slamming Nelson's chest with the paddles. Steckle leaned forward and placed the stethoscope against the body's heart.

"Nothing."

"Shit! Up to 360!" roared Labraccio.

"You got it!" answered Hurley.

"Clear!" Another zap of current bucked Nelson's body up off the gurney.

Again, Steckle placed the stethoscope against Nelson's chest.

"Nothing! I can't hear anything!"

He scrambled up the oak tree, paying no attention to the splinters of bark digging into his hands. All he could think of was getting away. Near the top, he stopped, out of breath and clinging to the trunk. Below him, he could hear the others getting closer; the boys were laughing. Nelson shrank back, trying to conceal himself in the cover of the leaves; maybe they wouldn't look up and see him.

But the excited barking around the roots of the tree was bringing them to the oak. Champ, he'd forgotten about Champ. The dog had nosed him out and was racing around and yelping, putting his front paws up on the trunk and barking up into the top of the tree, as though he'd treed some small animal like a raccoon. That's what Nelson was, a small treed animal.

The others had spotted him now, shouting with evil merriment, calling out his name and pelting him with childish insults. They started picking up stones; they were going to throw rocks at him. Stones began to rain upward, through the leaves of the trees, one or two of them glancing off his shoulder or chest. Nelson sobbed aloud, and clung more tightly to the limb. It was Billy he was most afraid of. Billy Mahoney was the best thrower of them all.

Rachel ran hastily into the lab, out of breath. In one instant, she saw the situation. The boys were working over him feverishly, but Nelson wasn't responding. The monitors were flatline.

"He called me! He's been dead over nine minutes!" she rasped, stripping off her overcoat.

"*Nine minutes?*" Steckle's eyes popped at the information.

But Labraccio didn't even look up, he was concentrating ferociously on Nelson. "All right, let's intubate."

Rachel grabbed up the laryngoscope and attempted to shove it down into Nelson's throat, attaching the air tube and beginning to pump air through it. But the air wouldn't pump.

"Damn it! I can't get air! The trachea's too tight!"

"Starting CPR!" cried Labraccio. "One-one-thousand, two-one-thousand, three-one-thousand, breathe, Nelson. C'mon, Nelson, breathe! Shit!"

"Try again!" urged Joe Hurley.

"One-one-thousand, two-one-thousand, three-one-thousand. Breathe, Nelson, breathe! It's not working!" yelled Labraccio. "Intertrachial with eppy into throat!" he ordered.

A shocked silence from the rest of the Flatliner team. What Labraccio was asking for was a radical procedure, way out. To inject epinephrine directly into Nelson's trachea was taking a big chance. On the other hand, just what exactly did they have to lose? Nelson Wright was obviously very dead already.

Billy Mahoney picked up a rock, slowly and carefully. He ran his hands over it. It was exactly the rock he was looking for, large and round and smooth. A great rock for throwing. He caressed it lovingly, then held it up for Nelson to see. He turned it in his hand, so that Nelson could see just how hard a stone it was, how well it would fly. And all the while he was laughing, laughing.

"No, Billy, don't!" sobbed Nelson, watching in horror. "Please, don't!" Champ was barking, the boys were mocking him, but all that nine-year-old Nelson could see was the rock in Billy Mahoney's hand. He knew with great clarity what would happen. He saw Billy's hand go back, saw the rock leave it, arching high into the air. . . .

"Billy, I'm sorry!" he screamed.

"Eppy in!" called Steckle. They were working as a team now, not competing, not getting in one another's way, just concentrating all their energies on the dead body on the gurney.

"One-one-thousand, two-one-thousand, three-one-thousand." Labraccio kept pumping hard on Nelson's bare chest. "Breathe, Nelson, come on and breathe!"

Steckle put the stethoscope against Nelson's heart and listened. "Nothing." Nothing had worked. It seemed hopeless, useless to go on. Nelson had been under far too long; there was no bringing him back.

"Get four milligrams of atropine ready," said Labraccio feverishly. He was sweating bullets, but he hadn't taken his eyes off Nelson. He was unaware that the others were now ready to give up.

Rachel looked at her wristwatch and winced. "David—"

He didn't look up from his CPR. "All right! Atropine intertracheal!" he commanded.

"This is a truckload full—" Randy Steckle protested.

"Never mind that. Do it!"

The long needle, with its powerful dose of stimulant, slid slowly into Nelson Wright's trachea.

"This has gotta work," gritted David through clenched teeth. His hair had tumbled forward over his brow, getting in his eyes, but he wasn't conscious of anything but Nelson. "Come on, Nelson. Come on. Come on. Come on." The words became a chant, and the others took it up unconsciously.

"Come on. Come on. Come on. Come on."

Nothing. Flatline.

* * *

"No, don't! Please, Billy, please don't!" The rock arched high in the air and came down through the branches, breaking off leaves as it fell. It hit Nelson squarely on the temple. He screamed, his head snapped back, and he lost his balance. Screaming and screaming, his arms flailing helplessly, he fell down through the tree, his terrified eyes seeing the ground below. At last, an eternity later, Nelson crashed to earth and lay still.

"He's been dead eleven minutes," said Steckle in a hushed voice. "It's hopeless."

"Eppy intracardial," Labraccio answered doggedly. He would not give up. Nelson was his friend, and you don't walk out on your friends.

"You're gonna kill him!" Joe protested loudly. A dose of stimulant directly into the heart muscle—it could rip the heart to pieces.

"Just do it!" snarled David.

Rachel picked up the syringe of epinephrine and hesitated, her eyes meeting Labraccio's. What she read there made her nod agreement. She plunged the needle of eppy directly into Nelson's heart. "Eppy in," she reported.

Nothing. Flatline.

Nelson Wright opened his eyes. He was lying on the ground, under the oak tree, and here was a very strange thing. He wasn't a boy anymore, he was a grown man. And he was dead, he knew that for certain. He was dead. He sat up, and saw a little boy in a red, hooded sweatshirt watching him. Billy Mahoney. They were both dead.

The boy raised his arms and put down the hood of his sweatshirt. It was Billy's face, but Nelson saw no fear in it, no anger. Only peace. Billy was at peace. Nelson had said he was sorry, and now Billy Mahoney was at peace. Atonement. Nelson had atoned with his life.

Champ was there, too. He was whole again, and not in pain. He stayed quietly and obediently at Billy's side.

Billy smiled at Nelson. The smile held a message. Death is peace. Death is good. Life is hard, but death is easy. Nelson smiled back. It seemed to him, too, that death was easier than life.

"He's been dead twelve minutes," said Steckle in a flat voice.

"One-one-thousand, two-one-thousand, three-one-thousand." Labraccio would not give up. "Four-one-thousand, *breathe*!"

"Forget it," Hurley said quietly. "He's dead. We lost him."

"*No*!" yelled Labraccio. He began to pound on Nelson's chest. Not CPR, but just a furious pounding. "You son of a bitch!" he shouted, weeping. "You son of a bitch!" He was totally out of control.

Horrified, Rachel reached out to him, pleading. "David! Stop it, David, stop it! David, let him go! You have to let him go! Stop it!" She reached for his hands, grabbed them in her own, forcing him to look at her.

Seeing her face, he realized at last that it was hopeless. Nelson was dead. David Labraccio drew in a deep and ragged breath, and let his hands lie limply in Rachel's for a moment. Then rage overtook him again, and he tore himself out of her clasp, pounding his fists on the wall in his frustrated fury. On the gurney, Nelson Wright lay very still, and the monitors showed flatlines. It was over.

"We're all responsible for this," said Randy Steckle.

"Maybe we deserve it," Joe Hurley said in a low tone.

Deserve it? Deserve *this*? "No!" shouted David. "No! It's not fair! It's not right!" He shook one angry fist at deaf Heaven, as men always do in the face of their injustices. "I'm sorry, God!" yelled the atheist. "I'm sorry we stepped on your fuckin' territory! Isn't that enough?!"

"Apparently not," Steckle said bitterly.

"Call the police," Hurley suggested.

Rachel struggled to keep from breaking down into weeping. "You know," she said huskily, "I could hear it in his voice. He felt he deserved to die."

"Bullshit!"

They turned in surprise. David Labraccio was coming back to the gurney, running, his face a thundercloud. "It was a mistake! He was a little kid, and *he doesn't deserve to die!*" He grabbed up the fully-charged defibrillator paddles.

"No!" It was a collective cry of horror, but it was too late. Before they could stop him, David slammed the defib paddles down on Nelson's chest. Hard. Four hundred joules of current zapped like a lightning strike through Nelson Wright's body. The body convulsed, rising high off the gurney and slamming violently back down.

A strong and very beautiful light blinded Nelson's eyes. Billy Mahoney turned and walked toward it, with Champ at his side. Before he reached it, he looked back at Nelson, and Nelson knew what it was Billy wanted. He was asking him to come, too. Forgiveness was total, and he could walk into the beautiful light with Billy and Champ and be at peace forever.

Nelson stood up. The light welcomed him, warmed him. He wanted to become a part of it. He took one step forward, then another. But suddenly, a loud noise off in the distance stopped him, and made him hesitate. In some deep part of himself, he knew what that sound was. It was the explosion of fully-charged defibrillator paddles against his own heart.

His time in the light with Billy and Champ would come much later, but he knew it would come, and that made Nelson happy. Now, it was time to go back.

"Charge! Clear!" announced David.

"No, wait!" Rachel cried. She had her ear

pressed hard against Nelson's chest, listening. And then she heard it, faint at first, but getting stronger. Nelson's heartbeat. "Oh, my God," she breathed.

"Get a pulse, get a pulse!" yelled Joe. They whirled as one and looked at the monitors. Both screens were blipping away, and the flatlines had become peaks and valleys. "We got him! We fuckin' got him!" A burst of incredulous happiness flooded through all of them.

"Don't rush him," Rachel cautioned, reaching for the oxygen mask. "Come on, Nelson, pick up the beat. Here we go, here we go." She put the mask on Nelson's face, and the four of them watched the miracle happen. The mask clouded a little with Nelson's feeble inhalations.

"That's it, he breathes." Labraccio smiled in satisfaction and pride. He was pleased with himself, pleased with all of them. They'd been doctors here tonight, real doctors. They'd done what doctors are supposed to do. They'd saved a human life.

"Take it easy," Rachel was crooning to Nelson. "That's right. Take it easy now."

Nelson opened his eyes. He looked around at the others and tried to smile, but he was still too weak. His eyes signaled David Labraccio that he wanted to say something, and Labraccio nodded, putting his ear to Nelson's parched lips. It was only a few whispered words.

"What did he say?" asked Joe Hurley.

"He said it wasn't such a good day to die," smiled David.

Nelson opened his mouth again. He smiled feebly at his friends. "Thank you," he whispered.

Outside the Dog Lab, in the sculpture that graced the rotunda, Man and Death were locked in a struggle for the possession of the wand of healing. Death's grip loosened, only a little.